D0934753

LITERATURE AND LANGUAGE DEPARTMENT
THE CHICAGO PUBLIC LIBRARY
400 SOUTH STATE STREET
CHICAGO, ILLINOIS 60605

A Rumpole Christmas

BY THE SAME AUTHOR

Charade

Rumming Park

Answer Yes or No

Like Men Betrayed

Three Winters

The Narrowing Stream

Will Shakespeare (An Entertainment)

Paradise Postponed

Summer's Lease

Titmuss Regained

Dunster

Felix in the Underworld

The Sound of Trumpets

Quite Honestly

Rumpole of the Bailey

The Trials of Rumpole

Rumpole for the Defence

Rumpole's Return

Rumpole and the Golden Thread

Rumpole's Last Case

Rumpole and the Age of Miracles

Rumpole à la Carte

Rumpole on Trial

The Best of Rumpole

Rumpole and the Angel of Death

Rumpole Rests His Case

Rumpole and the Primrose Path

Rumpole and the Penge Bungalow Murders

Rumpole and the Reign of Terror

Rumpole Misbehaves

Under the Hammer

With Love and Lizards
(with Penelope Mortimer)

Clinging to the Wreckage

Murderers and Other Friends

The Summer of a Dormouse

Where There's a Will

In Character

Character Parts

PLAYS

A Voyage Round My Father

The Dock Brief

What Shall We Tell Caroline?

The Wrong Side of the Park

Two Stars for Comfort

The Judge

Collaborators

Edwin, Bermondsey, Marble

Arch, Fear of Heaven

The Prince of Darkness

Naked Justice

Hock and Soda Water

A Rumpole Christmas

JOHN MORTIMER

Viking

VIKING
Published by the Penguin Group
Penguin Group (USA) Inc., 375 Hudson Street, New York, New York 10014, U.S.A.
Penguin Group (Canada), 90 Eglinton Avenue East, Suite 700, Toronto, Ontario, Canada M4P 2Y3
(a division of Pearson Penguin Canada Inc.) · Penguin Books Ltd, 80 Strand, London WC2R 0RL,
England · Penguin Ireland, 25 St. Stephen's Green, Dublin 2, Ireland (a division of Penguin Books
Ltd) · Penguin Books Australia Ltd, 250 Camberwell Road, Camberwell, Victoria 3124, Australia
(a division of Pearson Australia Group Pty Ltd) · Penguin Books India Pvt Ltd, 11 Community
Centre, Panchsheel Park, New Delhi – 110 017, India · Penguin Group (NZ), 67 Apollo Drive,
Rosedale, North Shore 0632, New Zealand (a division of Pearson New Zealand Ltd) · Penguin Books
(South Africa) (Pty) Ltd, 24 Sturdee Avenue, Rosebank, Johannesburg 2196, South Africa

Penguin Books Ltd, Registered Offices: 80 Strand, London WC2R 0RL, England

First published in 2009 by Viking Penguin, a member of Penguin Group (USA) Inc.

1   3   5   7   9   10   8   6   4   2

Copyright © Advanpress Ltd., 2009   All rights reserved

Page ix constitutes an extension of this copyright page.

Illustrations by Daniel Adel

Publisher's Note: This is a work of fiction. Names, characters, places, and incidents either are the
product of the author's imagination or are used fictitiously, and any resemblance to actual persons,
living or dead, business establishments, events, or locales is entirely coincidental.

LIBRARY OF CONGRESS CATALOGING IN PUBLICATION DATA
Mortimer, John, 1923–2009
A Rumpole Christmas / John Mortimer.
p. cm.
ISBN 978-0-670-02135-2
1. Rumpole, Horace (Fictitious character)—Fiction. 2. Detective and mystery stories, English.
3. London (England)—Fiction. 4. Christmas stories, English. I. Title.
PR6025.O7552R788 2009
823'.914—dc22   2009026816

Printed in the United States of America · Set in Adobe Garamond Pro · Designed by Amy Hill

Without limiting the rights under copyright reserved above, no part of this publication may be
reproduced, stored in or introduced into a retrieval system, or transmitted, in any form or by any
means (electronic, mechanical, photocopying, recording or otherwise), without the prior written
permission of both the copyright owner and the above publisher of this book.

The scanning, uploading, and distribution of this book via the Internet or via any other means
without the permission of the publisher is illegal and punishable by law. Please purchase only
authorized electronic editions and do not participate in or encourage electronic piracy of
copyrightable materials. Your support of the author's rights is appreciated.

Contents

Acknowledgements

"Rumpole and Father Christmas" was first published in the *Sunday Express* in 2005 and in *The Strand Magazine* in 2006. "Rumpole's Slimmed-Down Christmas" appeared under the title "Rumpole and the Health Farm Murder" in the *Daily Mail* in 2006 and under "Rumpole's Slimmed-Down Christmas" in *The Strand Magazine* in 2007. "Rumpole and the Boy" appeared in the *Daily Mail* in 1997. "Rumpole and the Old Familiar Faces" appeared in *The Strand Magazine* in 2001 and was also broadcast on BBC Radio Four in 2001. "Rumpole and the Christmas Break" appeared in *The Strand Magazine* in 2004 and in *Woman's Weekly* in 2004.

Rumpole and Father Christmas

Christmas had come again. There was tinsel and a few battered Christmas cards in the screws' room near the cells under the Old Bailey, you couldn't call on a tobacconist's for a packet of small cigars without being treated to a canned rendering of "God Rest Ye Merry Gentlemen" and, most unusually, our barristers' chambers at 4 Equity Court in the Temple was full of children.

The idea was Claude Erskine-Brown's, the opera-loving barrister whose twins, Tristan and Isolde, were then no more than seven years old. There were another four or five youngish barristers in our chambers at the time, all of whom had produced offspring, and old Uncle Tom, our oldest member, had unexpectedly contributed a couple of grandchildren. Mizz Liz Probert, my one-time pupil, had a niece, and extra children were bussed in from friendly chambers. It all seemed, with the streamers and games and going home presents, designed to arouse in these infants an early interest in lawyers and the law.

After much planning for the event, Claude had announced his final triumph to us at a chambers meeting. "I've had a bit of luck," he said. "I've managed to get Father Christmas for our children's party."

"Oh, congratulations, Erskine-Brown," I said. "What did you do? Travel to reindeer-land and bring him back on the Eurostar?"

"Don't be ridiculous, Rumpole. He's a fellow who advertises in the *Islington Gazette*." Here he produced a crumpled copy of the paper in question and read aloud, "Add a genuine Ho! Ho! Ho! to your Christmas party! A genuine and convincing Santa Claus is now accepting bookings." He added, "It gives a phone number in Palmers Green."

"Very few reindeer in Palmers Green," I suggested, having thought the matter over.

"Don't be silly, Rumpole. He hasn't got any reindeer."

"Hasn't he? You do surprise me."

"This is a fellow who has what is apparently a genuine talent for playing the part. And I've managed to secure his services."

Candidates for the party grew fast. Judge Bullingham (aka "The Mad Bull") called me into his room and asked if he could invite a couple of grandchildren. I consented, hoping that my generosity would dispose him towards keeping the Timson I was defending out of prison. Unfortunately, the spirit of peace and goodwill didn't move The Mad Bull to give my client community service. And so it was that a week or so before the Great Day, David Timson went to prison on a charge of receiving a huge quantity of Christmas puddings, amongst other things.

My wife, Hilda (known to me as She Who Must Be Obeyed), invited her old schoolfriend Laura Pewsey (who had no fewer than three daughters—all of whom were looking forward to the treat of meeting Claude's "genuine Santa") down from Yorkshire to stay in our mansion flat.

After a cold, bright day, darkness came early. As the gas lamps were being lit around the Temple, there was a ring at the door of our chambers. Our clerk, Henry, opened it to the "Ho! Ho! Ho!" of a figure who looked so like everyone's idea of Santa Claus that, perhaps after a glass or three of Château Thames Embankment, I might have believed the legend had come to life. He had exactly the right roundness of nose, his eye was bright and his flowing beard snowy white and he carried a voluminous bag—no doubt full of presents and other surprises. After another burst of "Ho! Ho! Ho!" he asked Henry if he might borrow our clerk's room to "prepare a few surprises." At the time it didn't occur to me to wonder why Santa would know about clerks' rooms in barristers' chambers.

The party assembled in the big room of our Head of Chambers, Sam Ballard, and there Father Christmas put on an excellent show. He conjured presents out of the air, told jokes, and persuaded the children to join him in a little song called "Does Santa Claus Sleep with His Whiskers Over or Under the Sheet?" Finally he invited questions from his juvenile audience.

The questions came thick and fast. Where did he put his reindeer when he came tonight? Did he really climb down chimneys? What did he do when he was young?

It was then that he started a long story about being brought up by gnomes, and as he conjured another present out of the air I noticed that half a finger was missing on his right hand. Suddenly the penny dropped and I saw another face behind the round red nose and the fake beard—a sharper, more eager and altogether greedier face. I put up my hand to ask a question.

"What do you remember of the Enfield Post Office job? Must be about twenty years ago now."

"Post Office?" Santa said in his Ho-ho-ish voice. "I must have stopped there to fill my sleigh with presents."

"Yes, of course," I said, and couldn't help adding, "I'm sure you did."

"I don't know why you asked him that ridiculous question," Hilda said after the party was over. She was going back with Laura to put the children to bed and she told me I'd have to look after myself until later.

Accordingly I went to Pommeroy's Wine Bar and thought about life with the help of a bottle of the old Château for a while, then went back to chambers. Around ten o'clock, I was surprised to hear a key turn in the front-door lock, followed by footsteps in the passageway. I waited for a minute and then emerged into the darkness and made for the clerk's room, from which odd noises had started emerging.

The lights were out but a lit torch lay on Henry's desk. By its light I saw the bulky figure of Santa Claus rummaging in his sack. He then pulled out a wadge of cheques and cash and placed them in the open desk drawer that Henry always kept locked—a precaution which had apparently proved no obstacle to this ingenious Santa.

"Fred Streeter," I said loudly as I switched on the light. "What the hell are you doing?"

"Putting your money back, Mr Rumpole," said the man I'd remembered as no more than a boy when he lost a finger breaking into the Enfield Post Office.

"You stole from us?"

"That was the idea, Mr Rumpole. You get lots of chances going into places as Father Christmas."

"What made you give it all back?"

"Just I remember you was kind to me, Mr Rumpole. You said I was led astray by my older cousins, who was real professional blaggers. You got me the minimum. When I saw you today, I remembered how grateful I'd been. So I came to put the cheques and that back."

"Was that the reason? Just seeing me again after all these years?"

"You weren't like the other briefs I'd dealt with before—those that treated me like a piece of dirt. You seemed really to care about me."

"Not enough to put you off the thieving."

"Perhaps not. It was a bit more than seeing you, though."

"What do you mean?"

"Well, all those kids were asking me questions about reindeers and all that ... I suppose I started to feel a bit mean about what I'd really come for. I had all these red clothes on, and the beard and that, but I also had your clerk's spare keys and all his cheques and petty cash in my bag. It hadn't struck me that way before. But then, well, suddenly it didn't seem right."

"You mean, the spirit of Christmas overcame you? You went for a little peace and goodwill towards men?"

"Is that what it was?" Father Christmas, otherwise known as Fred Streeter, looked puzzled.

"Most probably."

"That sort of thing doesn't usually get to me."

"Well, it seems it has."

"Mr Rumpole, why don't you put that in your Christmas stocking?" he said, handing me a folded slip of paper.

I looked at what he had given me. It was a cheque made out to me—my fee for some long-since closed Timson case. "Thank you," I said. "And a Happy Christmas to you."

"Ho! Ho! Ho!" said Fred, back in his role as Santa, as he returned the money and the spare keys to Henry's desk.

"I suppose you were drinking in that awful little wine bar of yours," Hilda said the next morning.

"Yes," I had to admit. "I was in Pommeroy's."

"Oh, Rumpole!" Hilda said as she chased down one of Laura's children who was storming round our flat. "When will you get in touch with the spirit of Christmas?"

"Don't talk to me about the spirit of Christmas," I warned her. "I've seen it at work, and it's extraordinary!"

Rumpole's Slimmed-Down Christmas

Christmas comes but once a year, and it is usually preceded by Christmas cards kept in the prison officers' cubby holes around the Old Bailey and "Away in a Manger" bleating through Boots, where I purchase for my wife Hilda (known to me as She Who Must Be Obeyed) her ritual bottle of lavender water, which she puts away for later use, while she gives me another tie which I add to my collection of seldom-worn articles of clothing. After the turkey, plum pudding and a bottle or two of Pommeroy's Château Thames Embankment I struggle to keep my eyes open during the Queen's Speech.

Nothing like this happened over the Christmas I am about to describe.

Hilda broke the news to me halfway through December. "I have booked us in for four days over Christmas, Rumpole, at Minchingham Hall."

What, I wondered, was she talking about? Did She Who Must have relatives at this impressive-sounding address?

I said, "I thought we'd spend this Christmas at home, as usual."

"Don't be ridiculous, Rumpole. Don't you ever think about your health?"

"Not really. I seem to function quite satisfactorily."

"You really think so?"

"Certainly. I can get up on my hind legs in court when the occasion demands. I can stand and cross-examine, or make a speech lasting an hour or two. I've never been too ill to do a good murder trial. Of course, I keep myself fortified by a wedge of veal and ham pie and a glass or two of Pommeroy's Very Ordinary during the lunchtime adjournment."

"Slices of pie and red wine, Rumpole. How do you think that makes you feel?"

"Completely satisfied. Until teatime, of course."

"Teatime?"

"I might slip into the Tastee-Bite on Fleet Street for a cup of tea and a slice of Dundee cake."

"All that does is make you fat, Rumpole."

"You're telling me I'm fat?" The thought hadn't really occurred to me, but on the whole it was a fair enough description.

"You're on the way to becoming obese," she added.

"Is that a more serious way of saying I'm fat?"

"It's a very serious way of saying it. Why, the buttons fly off your waistcoat like bullets. And I don't believe you could run to catch a bus."

"Not necessary. I go by Tube to the Temple Station."

"Let's face it, Rumpole, you're fat and you're going to do something about it. Minchingham Hall is the place for you," she said, sounding more and more like an advert. "So restful, you'll leave feeling marvellous. And now that you've finished the long fraud case . . ."

"You mean," I thought I was beginning to see the light, "this Minchingham place is a hotel?"

"A sort of hotel, yes."

Again I should have asked for further particulars, but it was time for the news so I merely said, "Well, I suppose it means you won't have to cook at Christmas."

"No, I certainly won't have to do that!" Here She Who Must gave a small laugh, that I can only describe as merciless, and added, "Minchingham Hall is a health farm, Rumpole. They'll make sure there's less of you by the time you leave. I've still got a little of the money Auntie Dot left me in her will and I'm going to give you the best and the healthiest Christmas you've ever had."

"But I don't need a healthy Christmas. I don't feel ill."

"It's not only your health, Rumpole. I was reading about it in a magazine at the hairdresser's. Minchingham Hall specializes in spiritual healing. It can put you in touch with yourself."

"But I've met myself already."

"Your *true* self, Rumpole. That's who you might find in 'the restful tranquillity of Minchingham Hall,'" she quoted from the magazine.

I wondered about my true self. Had I ever met him? What would he turn out to be like? An ageing barrister who bored on about his old cases? I hoped not—and if that was all he was, I'd rather not meet him. And as for going to the health farm, "I'll think it over," I told Hilda.

"Don't bother yourself, Rumpole," she said. "I've already thought."

"Tell me quite honestly, Mizz Probert," I said in the corridor in front of Number Six Court at the Old Bailey, "would you call me fat?"

Mizz Liz, a young barrister and my pupil, was defending Colin Timson who, in a pub fight with a rival gang, the

Molloys, was alleged to have broken a bottle and wounded Brian Molloy in the arm.

"No, I wouldn't call you that."

"Wouldn't you?" I gave her a grateful smile.

"Not to your face, I wouldn't. I wouldn't be so rude," Mizz Liz Probert replied.

"But behind my back?"

"Oh, I might say it then."

"That I'm fat?"

"Well, yes."

"But you've nothing against fat men?"

"Well, nothing much, I suppose. But I wouldn't want a fat boyfriend."

"You know what Julius Caesar said?"

"I've no idea."

"Let me have men about me that are fat; / Sleek-headed men and such as sleep o' nights."

Mizz Probert looked slightly mystified, and as the prosecuting counsel, Soapy Sam Ballard QC, the Head of our Chambers, approached, I went on paraphrasing Julius Caesar. "Yond Ballard has a lean and hungry look; / He thinks too much: such men are dangerous."

As Ballard came up I approached him. "Look here, Ballard, I've been meaning to talk to you about the Timson case," I said. "We all know the bottle broke and Brian Molloy fell on to it by accident. If we plead guilty to affray will you drop the grievous bodily harm?"

"Certainly not."

"But surely, Ballard, you could be generous. In the spirit of Christmas?"

"The spirit of Christmas has got nothing to do with your client fighting with a broken bottle."

"Goodwill and mercy to all men except Colin Timson. Is that it?"

"I'm afraid it is."

"You should go away somewhere to have your spiritual aura cleansed, Ballard. Spend Christmas somewhere like a health farm."

The result of all this was that the young Timson went to prison and I went to the health farm.

On Christmas Eve we took a train to Norwich and then a taxi across flat and draughty countryside (the wind, I thought, blew directly from the Russian Steppes, unbroken by any intervening mountains).

Minchingham, when we got there, appeared to be a village scattered around a grey-walled building that reminded me, irresistibly, of Reading Gaol. This was Minchingham Hall, the scene of this year's upcoming Christmas jubilations.

The woman at the reception desk was all grey—grey hair, grey face and a grey cardigan pulled down over her knuckles to keep her hands warm.

She told us that Oriana was giving someone a "treatment" and would be down soon to give us a formal welcome and to hug us.

"Did you say 'hug'?" I couldn't believe my ears.

"Certainly, Mr Rumpole. People travel here from all over England to be hugged by Oriana Mandeville. She'll suffuse you with 'good energy.' It's all part of the healing process. Do take a seat and make yourselves comfortable."

We made ourselves uncomfortable on a hard bench beside the cavernous fireplace and, in a probably far too loud whisper, I asked Hilda if she knew the time of the next train back to London.

"Please, Rumpole!" she whispered urgently. "You promised to go through with this. You'll see how much good it's going to do you. I'm sure Oriana will be with us in a minute."

Oriana was with us in about half an hour. A tall woman with a pale, beautiful face and a mass of curling dark hair, she was dressed in a scarlet shirt and trousers. This gave her a military appearance—like a female member of some revolutionary army. On her way towards us she glanced at our entry in the visitors' book on the desk and then swooped on us with her arms outstretched.

"The dear Rumbelows!" Her voice was high and enthusiastically shrill. "Helena and Humphrey. Welcome to the companionship of Minchingham Hall! I can sense that you're both going to respond well to the treatments we have on offer. Let me hug you both. You first, Helena."

"Actually, it's Hilda." Her faced was now forcibly buried in the scarlet shirt of the taller Oriana. Having released my wife her gaze now focused on me.

"And now you, Humphrey . . ."

"My first name's Horace," I corrected her. "You can call me Rumpole."

"I'm sorry. We're so busy here that we sometimes miss the details. Why are you so stiff and tense, Horace?" Oriana threw her arms around me in a grip which caused me to stiffen in something like panic. For a moment my nose seemed to be in her hair, but then she threw back her head, looked me straight in the eye and said, "Now we've got you here we're really going to teach you to relax, Horace."

We unpacked in a bedroom suite as luxurious as that in any other country hotel. In due course, Oriana rang us to invite us on a tour of the other, less comfortable attractions of Minchingham Hall.

There were a number of changing rooms where the visitors, or patients, stripped down to their underpants or knickers and, equipped with regulation dressing gowns and slippers, set out for their massages or other treatments. Each of these rooms, so Oriana told us, was inhabited by a "trained and experienced therapist" who did the pummelling.

The old building was centred around the Great Hall where, below the soaring arches, there was no sign of mediaeval revelry. There was a "spa bath"—a sort of interior whirlpool—and many mechanical exercise machines. Soft music played perpetually and the lights changed from cold blue to warm purple. A helpful blonde girl in white trousers and a string of beads came up to us.

"This is Shelagh," Oriana told us. "She was a conventional nurse before she came over to us and she'll be giving you most of your treatments. Look after Mr and Mrs Rumbelow, Shelagh. Show them our steam room. I've got to greet some new arrivals."

So Oriana went off, presumably to hug other customers, and Shelagh introduced us to a contraption that looked like a small moving walkway which you could stride down but which travelled in the opposite direction, and a bicycle that you could exhaust yourself on without getting anywhere.

These delights, Hilda told me, would while away the rest of my afternoon whilst she was going to opt for the relaxing massage and sunray therapy. I began to wonder, without much hope, if there were anywhere in Minchingham Hall where I could find something that would be thoroughly bad for me.

The steam room turned out to be a building—almost a small house—constructed in a corner of the Great Hall. Beside the door were various dials and switches which, Shelagh told us, regulated the steam inside the room.

"I'll give you a glimpse inside," Shelagh said, and she swung the door open. We were immediately enveloped in a surge of heat which might have sprung from an equatorial jungle. Through the cloud we could see the back of a tall, perspiring man wearing nothing but a towel around his waist.

"Mr Airlie!" Shelagh called into the jungle. "This is Mr and Mrs Rumpole. They'll be beginning their treatments tomorrow."

"Mr Rumpole. Hi!" The man turned and lifted a hand. "Join me in here tomorrow. You'll find it's heaven. Absolute heaven! Shut the door, Shelagh, it's getting draughty."

Shelagh shut the door on the equatorial rain forest and returned us to a grey Norfolk afternoon. I went back to my room and read Wordsworth before dinner. There may have been a lot wrong with the English countryside he loved so much—there was no wireless, no telephone, no central heating and no reliable bus service. But at least at that time they had managed to live without health farms.

Before dinner all the guests were asked to assemble in the Great Hall for Oriana to give us a greeting. If I had met myself at Minchingham Hall I also met the other visitors. The majority of them were middle-aged and spreading, as middle-aged people do, but there were also some younger, more beautiful women—who seemed particularly excited by the strange environment—and a few younger men.

Oriana stood, looking, I thought, even more beautiful than ever as she addressed us. "Welcome to you all on this Eve of Christmas and welcome especially to our new friends. When you leave you are going, I hope, to be more healthy than when you arrived. But there is something even more important than physical health. There is the purification of our selves so that we can look inward and find peace and tranquillity. Here at Minchingham we call that 'bliss.' Let us now enjoy a short period of meditation and then hug our neighbours."

I meditated for what seemed an eternity on the strange surroundings, the state of my bank balance and whether there was a chance of a decent criminal defence brief in the New Year. My reverie was broken by Oriana's command to hug. The middle-aged, fairly thin, balding man next to me took me in his arms.

"Welcome to Minchingham, Rumpole. Graham Banks. You may remember I instructed you long ago in a dangerous driving case."

It was the first time in my life that I'd been hugged by a

solicitor. As it was happening, Oriana started to hum and the whole company joined in, making a noise like a swarm of bees. There may have been some sort of signal, but I didn't see it, and we processed as one in what I hoped was the direction of the dining room. I was relieved to find that I was right. Perhaps things were looking up.

The dining room at Minchingham Hall was nowhere near the size of the Great Hall but it was still imposing. There was a minstrels' gallery where portraits hung of male and female members of the Minchingham family—who had inhabited the hall, it seemed, for generations before the place had been given over to the treatment industry.

Before the meal I was introduced to the present Lord Minchingham, a tall, softly spoken man in a tweed suit who might have been in his late fifties. His long nose, heavy eye-lids and cynical expression were echoed in the portraits on the walls.

"All my ancestors—the past inhabitants of Minching-ham Hall," he explained and seemed to be dismissing them with a wave of his hand. Then he pointed to a bronze angel with its wings spread over a map of the world as it was known in the seventeenth century. "This is a small item that might amuse you, Mr Rumpole. You see, my ancestors were great travellers and they used this to plan in which direction they would take their next journey," and he showed me how the angel could be swivelled round over the map. "At the moment I've got her pointing upwards as they may well be in heaven. At least, some of them."

When we sat down to dinner Hilda and I found ourselves at a table with Graham Banks (the solicitor who had taken me in his arms earlier) and his wife. Banks told us that he was Oriana's solicitor and he was at pains to let me know that he now had little to do with the criminal law.

"Don't you find it very sordid, Rumpole?" he asked me.

"As sordid and sometimes as surprising as life itself," I told him, but he didn't seem impressed.

Lord Minchingham also came to sit at our table, together with the corpulent man I had last seen sweating in the steam room, who gave us his name as Fred Airlie.

Dinner was hardly a gastronomic treat. The aperitif consisted of a strange, pale yellowish drink, known as "yak's milk." We were told it is very popular with the mountain tribes of Tibet. It may have tasted fine there, but it didn't, as they say of some of the finest wines, travel well. In fact it tasted so horrible that as I drank it I closed my eyes and dreamed of Pommeroy's Very Ordinary.

The main course, indeed the only course, was a small portion of steamed spinach and a little diced carrot, enough, perhaps, to satisfy a small rodent but quite inadequate for a human.

It was while I was trying to turn this dish, in my imagination, into a decent helping of steak and kidney pie with all the trimmings that I was hailed by a hearty voice from across the table.

"How are you getting on, Rumpole? Your first time here, I take it?" Fred Airlie asked me.

I wanted to say, "The first and, I hope, the last," but I restrained myself. "I'm not quite sure I need treatments," was what I said.

"The treatments are what we all come here for," Airlie boomed at me. "As I always say to Oriana, your treatments are our treats!"

"But fortunately I'm not ill."

"What's that got to do with it?"

"Well, I mean, it's bad enough being treated when you're ill. But to be treated when you're not ill . . ."

"It's fun, Rumpole. This place'll give you the greatest time in the world. Anyway, you look as though you could lose half a stone. I've lost almost that much."

"Ah! Is that so?" I tried to feign interest.

"You've come at a fortuitous moment," Airlie said. "Oriana is going to give us a special Christmas dinner."

"You mean turkey?"

"Turkey meat is quite low in calories," Airlie assured me.

"And bread sauce? Sprouts? Roast potatoes?"

"I think she'd allow a sprout. So cheer up, Rumpole."

"And Christmas pud?"

"She's found a special low calorie one. She's very pleased about that."

"Wine?" I sipped my glass of water hopefully.

"Of course not. You can't get low calorie wine."

"So the traditional Christmas cheer is, 'Bah, humbug.'"

"Excuse me?" Airlie looked puzzled.

"A touch of the Scrooge about the health farm manageress, is there?" It was no doubt rude of me to say it, and I wouldn't, probably, have uttered such a sacrilegious thought in those sanctified precincts if Oriana had been near.

For a moment or two Airlie sat back in his chair, regarding me with something like horror, but another voice came to my support.

"Looking around at my ancestors on these walls," Lord Minchingham murmured, as though he was talking to himself, "it occurs to me that they won several wars, indulged in complicated love affairs and ruled distant territories without ever counting the calories they consumed."

"But that was long ago," Airlie protested.

"It was indeed. Very, very long ago."

"You can't say Oriana lacks the Christmas spirit. She's decorated the dining room."

There were indeed, both in the dining room and the

Great Hall, odd streamers placed here and there and some sprigs of holly under some of the pictures. These signs had given me some hopes for a Christmas dinner, hopes that had been somewhat dashed by my talk with Airlie.

"In my great-grandfather's day," Minchingham's voice was quiet but persistent, "a whole ox was roasted on a spit in the Great Hall. The whole village was invited."

"I think we've rather grown out of the spit-roasting period, haven't we?" Airlie was smiling tolerantly. "And we take a more enlightened view of what we put in our mouths. Whatever you say about it, I think Oriana's done a wonderful job here. Quite honestly, I look on this place as my home. I haven't had much of a family life, not since I parted company with the third Mrs Airlie. This has become my home and Oriana and all her helpers are my family. So, Mr Rumpole, you're welcome to join us." Airlie raised his glass and took a swig of yak's milk, which seemed to give him the same good cheer and feeling of being at one with world as I got from a bottle of Château Thames Embankment.

"And let me tell you this." He leaned forward and lowered his voice to a conspiratorial whisper. "When I go, all I've got will go to Oriana, so she can build the remedial wing she's so keen on. I've told her that."

"That's very good of you." Minchingham seemed genuinely impressed. "My old father was very impressed with Oriana when he did the deal with her. But he wasn't as generous as you."

"I'm not generous at all. It's just a fair reward for all the good this place has done me." He sat back with an extremely satisfied smile.

I've always found people who talk about their wills in public deeply embarrassing, as though they were admitting to inappropriate love affairs or strange sexual behaviour. And then I thought of his lost half stone and decided it must have had enormous value to bring such a rich reward to the health farm.

Thomas Minchingham left us early. When he had gone, Airlie told us, "Tom Minchingham rates Oriana as highly as we all do. And, as he told us, his father did before him."

Whether it was hunger or being in a strange and, to me, curiously alien environment, I felt tired and went to bed early. Hilda opted for a discussion in the Great Hall on the "art of repose," led by two young men who had become Buddhist monks. I had fallen asleep some hours before she got back and, as a consequence, I woke up early.

I lay awake for a while as a dim morning light seeped through the curtains. My need for food became imperative and I thought I might venture downstairs to see if breakfast was still a custom at Minchingham Hall.

When I turned on the lights the dining room had been cleared and was empty. I thought I could hear sounds from the kitchen but I was stopped by a single cry, a cry of panic or a call for help. I couldn't tell which. I only knew that it was coming from the Great Hall.

When I got there, I saw the nurse Shelagh, already dressed, standing by the door to the steam room. The door was open and hot steam was billowing around. Looking into the room I saw Fred Airlie lying face down; a pool of blood had formed under his forehead.

Shelagh came towards me out of the mist.

"Is he hurt badly?" I asked her.

"Is he hurt?" she repeated. "I'm afraid he's dead. He couldn't get out, you see."

"Why couldn't he? The door opens . . ."

Shelagh bent down and picked up a piece of wood, about a foot long; it could have been part of a sawn-off chair leg. As she held it out to me she said, "Someone jammed the door handle with this on the outside. That's how I found it when I came down."

She showed me how the wood had been jammed into the oval circle of the door handle. Fred Airlie had been effectively locked into a steam-filled tomb and left there to die.

"I think you'd better call someone, don't you?" I said to Shelagh. She agreed and went at once to the small closet that held the telephone. I waited for her to come back and, once she arrived, told her that I was going to my room and would make myself available if needed.

It was Christmas morning. The bells of the village church rang out the usual peals of celebration. The sun rose cheerfully, flecking the empty branches of the trees with an unusually golden light. In our bedroom Hilda and I exchanged presents. I received my tie and socks with appropriate gasps of surprise and delight and she greeted her lavender water in the same way. It was difficult to remember that, in the apparently peaceful health farm, a man had been done horribly to death while we were asleep.

"I don't know what it is about you, Rumpole," She Who Must Be Obeyed told me, "but you do seem to attract crime wherever you go. You often say you're waiting for some good murder case to come along."

"Do I say that?" I felt ashamed.

"Very often."

"I suppose that's different," I tried to excuse myself. "I get my work long after the event. Served up cold in a brief. There are names, photographs of people you've never met. It's all laid out for a legal argument. But we had dinner with Fred Airlie. He seemed so happy," I remembered.

"Full of himself." He had clearly failed to charm She Who

Must Be Obeyed. "When you go downstairs, Rumpole, just you try to keep out of it. We're on holiday, remember, and it's got absolutely nothing to do with you."

When I got downstairs again there was a strange and unusual quietness about the Great Hall and the dining room. The steam-room door was closed and there was a note pinned to it that said it was out of order. A doctor had been sent for and had gone away after pronouncing Airlie dead. An ambulance had called and removed the body.

Oriana was going around her patients and visitors, doing her best to spread calm. As I sat down to breakfast (fruit, which I ate, and special low calorie muesli, which I avoided) Graham Banks, the solicitor, came and sat down beside me. He seemed, I thought, curiously enlivened by the night's events. However, he began by accusing me of a personal interest.

"I suppose this is just up your street, isn't it, Rumpole?"

"Not really. I wouldn't want that to happen to anyone," I told him.

Banks thought this over and poured himself a cup of herbal tea (the only beverage on offer). "You know that they're saying someone jammed the door so Airlie couldn't escape?"

"Shelagh told me that."

"They must have done it after midnight when everyone else was asleep."

"I imagine so."

"Airlie often couldn't sleep so he took a late-night steam bath. He told me that, so he must have told someone else. Who, I wonder?"

"Yes. I wonder too."

"So someone must have been about, very early in the morning."

"That would seem to follow."

There was a pause then, whilst Banks seemed to think all this over. Then he said, "Rumpole, if they find anyone they think is to blame for this . . ."

"By 'they' you mean the police?"

"They'll have to be informed, won't they?" Banks seemed to be filled with gloom at the prospect.

"Certainly they will. And as the company's solicitor, I think you're the man to do it," I told him.

"If they suspect someone, will you defend them, whoever it is?"

"If I'm asked to, yes."

"Even if they're guilty?"

"They won't be guilty until twelve honest citizens come back from the jury room and pronounce them so. In this country we're still hanging on to the presumption of innocence, if only by the skin of our teeth."

There was a silence for a while as Banks got on with his

breakfast. Then he asked me, "Will I have to tell them what Airlie said about leaving his money to Oriana?"

"If you think it might be relevant."

The solicitor thought this over quietly whilst he chewed his spoonful of low calorie cereal. Then he said, "The truth of the matter is that Minchingham Hall's been going through a bit of a bad patch. We've spent out on a lot of new equipment and the amount of business has been, well, all I can say is, disappointing. We're not really full up this Christmas. Of course, Oriana's a wonderful leader, but not enough people seem to really care about their health."

"You mean they cling to their old habits, like indulging in turkey with bread sauce and a few glasses of wine?" I couldn't resist the jab.

He ignored me. "The fact is, this organization is in desperate need of money."

I let this information hang in the air and we sat in silence for a minute or two, until Graham Banks said, "I was hungry during the night."

"I know exactly what you mean." I began to feel a certain sympathy for the solicitor.

"My wife was fast asleep so I thought I'd go down to the kitchen and see if they'd left anything out. A slice of cheese or something. What are you smiling at?"

"Nothing much. It's just so strange that well-off citizens like you will pay good money to be reduced to the hardships of the poor."

"I don't know about that. I only know I fancied a decent slice of cheese. I found some in the kitchen, and a bit of cake."

"Did you really? Does that mean that the kitchen staff are allowed to become obese?"

"I only know that when I started back up the stairs I met Oriana coming down." He was silent then, as if he was already afraid that he'd said too much.

"What sort of time was that?" I asked him.

"I suppose it was around one in the morning."

"Had she been to bed?"

"I think so. She was in a dressing gown."

"Did she say anything?"

"She said she'd heard some sort of a noise and was going down to see if everything was all right."

"Did you help her look?"

"I'm afraid not. I went straight on up to bed. I suddenly felt tired."

"It must have been the unexpected calories."

"I suppose so."

Banks fell silent again. I waited to see if there was going to be more. "Is that it?" I asked.

"What?"

"Is that all you want to tell me?"

"Isn't it enough?" He looked up at me, I thought pleadingly. "I need your advice, Rumpole. Should I tell the police all that? After all, I'm a friend of Oriana's. I've known her and been her friend for years. I suppose I'll have to tell them?"

I thought that with friends like that Oriana hardly needed enemies. I knew that the solicitor wouldn't be able to keep his story to himself. So I told him to tell the police what he thought was relevant and see what they would make of it. I was afraid I knew what their answer would be.

Someone, I wasn't sure who at the time, had been in touch with the police and two officers were to come at two thirty to interview all the guests. Meanwhile two constables were sent to guard us. Hilda and I wanted to get out of what had now become a Hall of Doom and I asked for, and got, permission to walk down to the village. The young officer in charge seemed to be under the mistaken impression that barristers don't commit murder.

Minchingham village was only half a mile away but it seemed light years from the starvation, the mechanical exercises and the sudden deathtrap at the Hall. The windows of the cottages were filled with Christmas decorations and children were running out of doors to display their presents. We went into the Lamb and Flag and made our way past a Christmas tree, into the bar. There was something here that had been totally absent at Minchingham Hall—the smell of cooking.

Hilda seemed pleased to be bought a large gin and tonic. Knowing that the wine on offer might be even worse than Pommeroy's, I treated myself to a pint of stout.

"We don't have to be back there till two thirty," I told her.

"I wish we never had to be back."

I felt for She Who Must in her disappointment. The visit to Minchingham Hall, designed to produce a new slim and slender Rumpole, had ended in disaster. I saw one positive advantage to the situation.

"While we're here anyway," I said, "we might as well have lunch."

"All right," Hilda sighed in a resigned sort of way. "If you don't *mind* being fat, Rumpole."

"I suppose I could put up with it," I hoped she realized I was facing the prospect heroically, "for another few years. Now, looking at what's chalked up on the blackboard, I see that they're offering steak pie, but you might go for the pizza."

It was while we were finishing our lunch that Thomas

Minchingham came into the pub. He had some business with the landlord and then he came over to our table, clearly shaken by the turn of events.

"Terrible business," he said. "It seems that the police are going to take statements from us."

"Quite right," I told him. "We're on our way back now."

"You know, I never really took to Airlie, but poor fellow, what a ghastly way to die. Shelagh rang and told me the door was jammed from the outside."

"That's right. Somebody did it."

"I suppose it might be done quite easily. There's all that wood lying around in the workshop. Anyone could find a bit of old chair leg . . . I say, would you mind if I joined you? It's all come as the most appalling shock."

"Of course not."

So His Lordship sat and consumed the large brandy he'd ordered. Then he asked, "Have they any idea who did it?"

"Not yet. They haven't started to take statements. But when they find out who benefits from Airlie's will, they might have their suspicions."

"You don't mean Oriana?" he asked.

"They may think that."

"But Oriana? No! That's impossible."

"Nothing's impossible," I said. "It seems she was up in the night. About the time Airlie took his late-night steaming. Her solicitor, Graham Banks, was very keen to point out all the evidence against her."

Minchingham looked shocked, thought it over and said, "But *you* don't believe it, do you, Mr Rumpole?"

"I don't really believe anything until twelve honest citizens come back from the jury room and tell me that it's true." I gave him my usual answer.

The Metropolitan Police call their country comrades "turnips," on the assumption that they are not very bright and so incapable of the occasional acts of corruption that are said to demonstrate the superior ingenuity of the "townees."

I suppose they might have called Detective Inspector Britwell a turnip. He was large and stolid with a trace of that country accent that had almost disappeared in the area around Minchingham. He took down statements slowly and methodically, licking his thumb as he turned the pages in his notebook. I imagined he came from a long line of Britwells who were more used to the plough and the axe than the notebook and pencil. His sidekick, Detective Sergeant Watkins, was altogether more lively, the product, I imagined, of a local sixth form college and perhaps a university. He would comment on his superior's interviews with small sighs and tolerant smiles and he occasionally contributed useful questions.

They set up their headquarters in the dining hall, far from the treatment area, and we waited outside for our turns.

Graham Banks was called first and I wondered if he would volunteer to be the principal accuser. When he came out he avoided Oriana, who was waiting with the rest of us, and went upstairs to join his wife.

Thomas Minchingham was called in briefly and I imagined that he was treated with considerable respect by the turnips. Then Shelagh went in to give the full account of her discovery of Airlie and the steam-room door.

Whilst we were waiting Oriana came up to me. She seemed, in the circumstances, almost unnaturally calm, as though Airlie's murder was nothing but a minor hitch in the smooth running of Minchingham Hall. "Mr Rumpole," she began. "I'm sorry I got your name wrong. Graham has told me you are a famous barrister. He says you are something of a legend around the courts of justice."

"I'm glad to say that I have acquired that distinction," I told her modestly, "since the day, many years ago, when I won the Penge Bungalow murder case alone and without a leader."

There was a moment's pause as she thought it over. I looked at her, a tall, rather beautiful woman, dedicated to the healing life, who was, perhaps a murderess.

"I'm entitled to have a lawyer present, when I'm answering their questions?"

"Certainly."

"Can I ask you to be my lawyer, Mr Rumpole?"

"I would have to be instructed by a solicitor."

"I've already spoken to Graham. He has no objections."

"Very well, then. You're sure you don't want Graham to be present as well?"

"Would you, Mr Rumpole," she gave a small, I thought rather bitter, smile, "in all the circumstances?"

"Very well," I agreed. "But in any trial I might be a possible witness. After all, I did hear what Airlie said. I might have to ask the judge's permission . . ."

"Don't let's talk about any trial yet." She put a slim hand on mine and her smile became sweeter. "I would like to think you were on my side."

I was called next into the dining room and the turnip in charge looked hard at me and said, without a smile, "I suppose you'll be ready to defend whoever did this horrible crime, Mr Rumpole."

"In any trial," I told him, "I try to see that justice is done." I'm afraid I sounded rather pompous and my remark didn't go down too well with the Detective Inspector.

"You barristers are there to get a lot of murderers off. That's been our experience down here in what you'd call 'the sticks.'"

"We are there to make an adversarial system work," I told

him, "and as for Minchingham, I certainly wouldn't call it 'the sticks.' A most delightful village, with a decent pub to its credit."

When I had gone through what I remembered of the dinner time conversation, the DI said they would see Oriana next.

"She has asked me to stay here with her," I told the DI, "as her legal representative."

There was a silence as he looked at me, and he finally said, "We thought as much."

Oriana gave her statement clearly and well. The trouble was that it did little to diminish or contradict the evidence against her. Yes, the Minchingham Hall health farm was in financial difficulties. Yes, Airlie had told her he was leaving her all his money, and she didn't improve matters by adding that he had told her that his estate, after many years as a successful stockbroker, amounted to a considerable fortune. Yes, she got up at about one in the morning because she thought she heard a noise downstairs, but, no, she didn't find anything wrong or see anybody. She passed the steam room and didn't think it odd that it was in use as Airlie would often go into it when he couldn't sleep at night. No, she saw nothing jamming the door and she herself did nothing to prevent the door being opened from the inside.

At this point the Detective Sergeant produced the chair

leg, which was now carefully wrapped in cellophane to preserve it as the prosecution's Exhibit A. The DI asked the
question.

"This was found stuck through the handle of the door to
the steam room. As you know, the door opens inwards so
this chair leg would have jammed the door and Mr Airlie
could not have got out. And the steam dial was pushed up
as high as it would go. Did you do that?"

Oriana's answer was a simple, "No."

"Do you have any idea who did?"

"No idea at all."

It was at this point that she was asked if she would agree
to have her fingerprints taken. I was prepared to make an
objection, but Oriana insisted that she was quite happy to
do so. The deed was done. I told the officers that I had seen
the chair leg for a moment when the nurse showed it to me,
but I hadn't held it in my hand, so as not to leave my own
prints on it.

At this DI Britwell made what I suppose he thought was
a joke. "That shows what a cunning criminal you'd make,
Mr Rumpole," he said, "if you ever decided to go on to the
wrong side of the law."

The DI and the DS laughed at this and once more Oriana gave a faintly amused smile. The turnips told us that
they planned to be back again at six p.m. and that until then

the witnesses would be carefully guarded and would not be allowed to leave the hall.

"And that includes you this time, Mr Rumpole," Detective Inspector Britwell was pleased to tell me.

Oriana made a request. A school choir with their music master were coming to sing carols at four o'clock. Would they be allowed in? Rather to my surprise DI Britwell agreed, no doubt infected by the spirit of Christmas.

As I left the dining room I noticed that the little baroque angel had been swivelled round. She was no longer pointing vaguely upward, and her direction now was England, perhaps somewhere in the area of Minchingham Hall.

The spirit of Christmas seemed to descend on Minchingham more clearly during that afternoon than at any other time during our visit. The Great Hall was softly lit, the Christmas decorations appeared brighter, the objects of exercise were pushed into the shadows, the choir had filed in and the children's voices rose appealingly.

"Silent night," they sang, "holy night, / All is calm, all is bright, / Round yon Virgin Mother and Child / Holy Infant so tender and mild / Sleep in heavenly peace . . ."

I sat next to Shelagh the nurse, who was recording the children's voices on a small machine. "Just for the record," she said. "I like to keep a record of all that goes on in the hall."

A wonderful improvement, I thought, on her last recorded event. And then, because the children were there, we were served Christmas tea, and a cake and sandwiches were produced. It was a golden moment when Minchingham Hall forgot the calories!

When it was nearly six o'clock Detective Inspector Britwell arrived. He asked me to bring Oriana into the dining hall and I went with her to hear the result of any further action he might have taken. It came, shortly and quickly.

"Oriana Mandeville," he said. "I am arresting you for the wilful murder of Frederick Alexander Airlie. Anything you say may be taken down and used in evidence at your trial . . ."

I awoke very early on Boxing Day, when only the palest light was seeping through a gap in the curtains. The silent night and holy night was over. It was time for people all over the country to clear up the wrapping paper, put away the presents, finish up the cold turkey and put out tips for the postman. Boxing Day is a time to face up to our responsibilities. My wife, in the other twin bed, lay sleeping peacefully. Hilda's responsibilities didn't include the impossible defence of a client charged with murder when all the relevant evidence seemed to be dead against her.

I remembered Oriana's despairing, appealing look as Detective Inspector Britwell made her public arrest. "You'll get me out of this, won't you?" was what the look was saying, and at that moment I felt I couldn't make any promises.

I bathed, shaved and dressed quietly. By the time I went downstairs it had become a subdued, dank morning, with black, leafless trees standing against a grey and unsympathetic sky.

There seemed to be no one about. It was as if all the guests, overawed by the tragedy that had taken place, were keeping to their rooms in order to avoid anything else that might occur.

I went into the echoing Great Hall, mounted a stationary bike and started pedalling on my journey to nowhere at all. I was trying to think of any possible way of helping Oriana at her trial. Would I have to listen to the prosecution witnesses and then plead guilty in the faint hope of getting the judge to give my client the least possible number of years before she might be a candidate for parole? Was that all either she or I could look forward to?

I had just decided that it was when I heard again, in that empty hall, the sound of the children's voices singing "Once in Royal David's City." I got off the bike and went to one of the treatment rooms. Nurse Shelagh was alone there, sitting on a bed and listening to her small tape recorder.

When she saw me she looked up and wiped the tears from her eyes with the knuckles of her hands. She said,

"Forgive me, Mr Rumpole. I'm being silly." And she switched off the music.

"Not at all," I told her. "You've got plenty to cry about."

"She told me you're a famous defender. You'll do all you can for her, won't you, Mr Rumpole?"

"All I can. But it might not be very much."

"Oriana wouldn't hurt anyone. I'm sure of that."

"She's a powerful woman. People like her are continually surprising."

"But you will do your best, won't you?"

I looked at Shelagh, sadly unable to say much to cheer her up. "Could you turn me into a slim, slender barrister in a couple of days?" I asked her.

"Probably not."

"There, you see. We're both playing against impossible odds." I picked up the small recording machine. "Is this what you used to record the children?" It was about as thick as a cigarette packet but a few inches longer.

"Yes. Isn't it ridiculous? It's the Dictaphone we use in the office. It's high time we got some decent equipment."

"Don't worry," I said, as I gave it back to her. "Everything that can be done for Oriana will be done."

The dining hall was almost empty at breakfast time, but I heard a call of "Rumpole! Come and join us." So I reluctantly went to sit down with Graham Banks, the solicitor, and his wife. I abolished all thoughts of bacon and eggs and tucked into a low calorie papaya biscuit. I rejected the yak's milk on this occasion in favour of a pale and milk-less tea.

"She wants you to represent her," Banks began.

"That's what she told me."

"So I'll be sending you a brief, Rumpole. But of course she's in a hopeless situation."

I might have said, "She wouldn't be in such a hopeless situation if you hadn't handed over quite so much evidence to help the police in their conviction of your client's guilt." But I restrained myself and only said, "You feel sure she's the one who did it?"

"Of course. She was due to inherit all Airlie's money. Who else had a motive?"

"I can't think of anyone at the moment."

"If she's found guilty of murdering Airlie she won't be able to inherit the money anyway. That's the law, isn't it?"

"Certainly."

"I'll have to tell her that. Then there'd be no hope of the health farm getting the money either. Tom Minchingham's father made the contract with her personally."

"Then you've got a bundle of good news for her." I dug into what was left of my papaya biscuit.

"There is another matter." Banks looked stern. "I'll also have to tell her that the prosecution will probably oppose bail because of the seriousness of the offence."

"More good news," I said, but this time the solicitor ignored me and continued to look determinedly grave and hopeless. At this point Mrs Banks announced that they were going straight back to London. "This place is now too horrible to stay in for a moment longer."

"Are you going back to London this morning, Rumpole?" Banks asked me.

"Not this morning. I might stay a little while longer. I might have a chat with some of the other people who were with us at the table with Airlie."

"Whatever for?"

"Oh, they might have heard something helpful."

"Can you imagine what?"

"Not at the moment."

"Anyway," Graham Banks gave me a look of the utmost severity, "it's the solicitor's job to go around collecting the evidence. You won't find any other barrister doing it!"

"Oh, yes, I know." I did my best to say this politely. "But then I'm not any other barrister, am I?"

It turned out that She Who Must Be Obeyed was of one mind with Mrs Banks. "I want to get out of here as quickly as possible," she said. "The whole Christmas has been a complete disaster. I shall never forget the way that horrible woman killed that poor man."

"So you're giving up on health farms?"

"As soon as possible."

"So I can keep on being fat?"

"You may be fat, Rumpole, but you're alive! At least that can be said for you."

I asked Hilda for her recollection of the dinner-table conversation, which differed only slightly from my own memory and that of Banks and his wife. There was another, slim, young couple at our table, Jeremy and Anna, who were so engrossed in each other that they had little recall of what else had been going on. The only other person present was Tom Minchingham.

I obtained his number from Shelagh and I rang him. I told him what I wanted and suggested we discuss it over a bottle of wine in the dining hall.

"Wine? Where do you think you're going to find that at the health farm?"

"I took the precaution of placing a bottle in my hand luggage. It's vintage Château Thames Embankment. I feel sure you'd like it."

He told me that it would have to be in the afternoon, so I said that would suit me well.

After lunch was over and the table had been cleared I set

out the bottle and two glasses. I also moved a large and well-covered potted plant nearer to where we were going to sit.

Then I made a brief call to Shelagh and received a satisfactory answer to the question I should have asked earlier. I felt a strange buzz of excitement at the almost too late understanding of a piece of the evidence in Oriana's case which should have been obvious to me. Then I uncorked the bottle and waited as calmly as I could for the arrival of the present Lord Minchingham.

He arrived, not more than twenty minutes late, in a politely smiling mood. "I'm delighted to have a farewell drink with you, Rumpole," he said. "But I'm afraid I can't help you with this ghastly affair."

"Yes," I said. "It's very ghastly."

"It's terrible to think of such a beautiful woman facing trial for murder."

"It's terrible to think of anyone facing trial for murder."

"You know, something about Oriana has the distinct look of my ancestor Henrietta Ballantyne, as she was before she became Countess Minchingham. There she is, over the fireplace."

I turned to see the portrait of a tall, beautiful woman dressed in grey silk, with a small spaniel at her feet. She had none of Oriana's features except for a look of undisputed authority.

"She married the fourth earl in the reign of James the Second. It was well known that she took lovers, and they all died in mysterious circumstances. One poisoned, another stabbed in the dark on his way home from a ball. Another drowned in a mill stream."

"What was the evidence against her?"

"Everyone was sure she was guilty."

"Perhaps her husband did it."

"He was certainly capable of it. He is said to have strangled a stable lad with his bare hands because his favourite mare went lame. But the countess certainly planned the deaths of her lovers. You're not going to defend her as well, are you, Rumpole? It's a little late in the day to prove my dangerous ancestor innocent."

"What happened to her?"

"She lived to the age of eighty. An extraordinary attainment in those days. Her last three years were spent as a nun."

"As you say, a considerable attainment," I agreed. "Shall we drink to her memory?"

I filled our glasses with Château Thames Embankment. His Lordship drank and pulled a face. "I say, this is a pretty poor vintage, isn't it?"

"Terrible," I told him. "There is some impoverished area of France, a vineyard perhaps, situated between the pissoir and the barren mountain slopes, where the Château Thames

Embankment grape struggles for existence. Its advantages are that it is cheap and it can reconcile you to the troubles of life and even, in desperate times, make you moderately drunk. Can I give you a refill?"

In spite of his denigration of the vintage Lord Minchingham took another glass. "Are you well known for taking on hopeless cases, Rumpole?" he asked me, when his glass was empty.

"Some people might say that of me."

"And I should think they may be damned right. First of all you want to defend my ancestor, who's dead, and now I hear you've taken on the beautiful Oriana, who is clearly guilty."

"You think that, do you?"

"Well, isn't it obvious?"

I poured myself another glass and changed the subject. "You're devoted to this house, aren't you?"

"Well, it does mean a lot to me. It's the home of my ancestors. Their portraits are on the walls around us. If they could speak to us, God knows what they would say about the present occupants."

"You don't think that the health farm should be here?"

"You want me to be honest, Rumpole?"

"Yes," I said. "I'd like you to be that."

"This house has been in my family since Queen Elizabeth made one of her young courtiers the first Earl of

Minchingham, probably because she rather fancied him. I don't say that my ancestors had any particular virtues, Rumpole, but they have been part of British history. We fought for the King in the Civil War. We led a regiment at Waterloo. We went out and ruled bits of the British Empire. One was a young brigadier killed on the Somme. I suppose most of them would have fancied Oriana, but not as a marriage proposition. But as for the rest of the people here, I don't think there's a chance that any one of them would have received an invitation to dinner."

"Do you think they would have invited me to dinner?"

There was a pause and then he said, "If you want me to be completely honest, Rumpole, no."

"Didn't they need lawyers?"

"Oh, yes. They needed them in the way they needed gamekeepers and carpenters and butlers and cooks. But they didn't invite them to dinner."

I considered this and refilled our glasses. "I suppose you think your old father did the wrong thing, then?"

"Of course he did. I suppose he became obsessed with Oriana."

"Did you argue with him about it?"

"I was away in the army at the time. He sent me a letter, after the event. I just couldn't believe what he'd done."

"How did he meet Oriana?"

"Oh, she had some sort of health club in London. A friend recommended it to him. I think she cured his arthritis. It couldn't have been very bad arthritis, could it?"

I couldn't help him about his father's arthritis, so I said nothing.

"I imagine he fell in love with her. So he gave her this— all our history."

"But she must have been paying for it. In rent."

"Peanuts. He must have been too besotted when he signed the contract."

We had got to a stage in the conversation where I wanted to light a small cigar. Lord Minchingham told me that I was breaking all the rules.

"I feel the heart has been taken out of the health farm," I told him.

"Good for you. I hope it has."

"I can understand how you must feel. Where do you live now?"

"My father also sold the Dower House. He did that years ago, when my grandmother died. I live in one of the cottages in the village. It's perfectly all right but it's not Minchingham Hall."

"I can see what you mean."

"Can you? Can you really, Rumpole?" He seemed grateful for my understanding. "I'm afraid I haven't been much help to you."

"Don't worry. You've been an enormous help."

"We all heard what Airlie said at dinner. That he was leaving his fortune to Oriana."

"Yes," I agreed. "We all heard that."

"So I suppose that's why she did it."

"That's the generally held opinion," I told him. "The only problem is, of course, that she didn't do it."

"Is that what she's going to say in court?"

"Yes."

"No one will believe her."

"On the contrary. Everyone will believe she didn't do it."

"Why?" Lord Minchingham laughed, a small, mirthless laugh, mocking me.

"Shelagh told me what she found. The steam turned up from the outside and a chair leg stuck through the door handle to stop it opening from the inside."

"So that's how Oriana did the murder."

"Do you really think that if she'd been the murderer she'd have left the chair leg stuck in the handle? Do you think she'd have left the steam turned up? Oriana may have her faults but she's not stupid. If she'd done it she'd have removed the chair leg and turned down the steam. That would have made it look like an accident. The person who did it wanted it to look like murder."

"Aren't you forgetting something?"

"What am I forgetting?"

"No one else would want to kill Airlie."

"Oh, Airlie wasn't considered important by whoever did this. Airlie was just a tool, like the chair leg in the door handle and the steam switch on the outside. If you want to know which victim this murderer was after, it wasn't Airlie, it was Oriana."

"Then who could it possibly be?"

"Someone who wanted Oriana to be arrested, and tried for murder. Someone who would be delighted if she got a life sentence. Someone who thought the health farm wouldn't exist without her. I haven't seen the contract she signed with your father. Did his lawyer put in some clause forbidding indecent or illegal conduct on the premises? In fact, Lord Minchingham, someone who desperately wanted his family home back."

The effect of this was extraordinary. As he sat at the table in front of me Tom Minchingham was no longer a cheerful, half-amused aristocrat. His hand gripped his glass and his face was contorted with rage. He seemed to have turned, before my eyes, into his ancestor who had strangled a stable lad with his bare hands.

"She deserved it," he said. "She had it coming! She cheated my father and stole my house from me!"

"I knew it was you," I told him, "when we met in the

pub. You talked about the chair leg in the door handle. When Shelagh rang you, she never said anything about a chair leg. She told me that. I suppose you've still got a key to the house. Anyway, you got in after everyone had gone to bed. Airlie told us at dinner about his late-night steam baths. You found him in there, enjoying the steam. Then you jammed the door and left him to die. Now Oriana's in an overnight police cell, I suppose you think your plan has been an uncommon success."

In the silence that followed Tom Minchingham relaxed. The murderous ancestor disappeared, the smiling aristocrat returned. "You can't prove any of it," he said.

"Don't be so sure."

"You can invent all the most ridiculous defences in the world, Mr Rumpole. I'm sure you're very good at that. But they won't save Oriana because you won't be able to prove anything. You're wasting my time and yours. I have to go now. I won't thank you for the indifferent claret and I don't suppose we will ever meet again."

He left then. When he had gone I retrieved, from the foliage of the potted plant on the table, the small Dictaphone I had borrowed from Shelagh. I felt as I always did when I sat down after a successful cross-examination.

Going home on the train, Hilda said, "You look remarkably pleased with yourself, Rumpole."

"I am," I said, a little cheered.

"And yet you haven't lost an ounce."

"I may not have lost an ounce but I've gained a defence brief. I think, in the case of the Queen versus Oriana, we might be able to defeat the dear old Queen.'

Rumpole and the Boy

The season of peace and goodwill to men was fast approaching. They'd turned on the carol tape in the Tastee-Bite where I took a simple breakfast of egg, bacon and fried slice. There were nodding reindeer and smiling Santas in the windows of the computer shops in Fleet Street and, down at the Old Bailey, I was engaged in a rather jolly little case of demanding money with menaces, more commonly known as "blackmail."

My client, perched in the dock, was a certain Maureen O'Keefe, who described herself as a "model," although the days when she strutted, slim as a rail, down any catwalk must have been distant. She now had a figure best described as comfortable, blonde hair that was darker at the roots, bitten fingernails and a smile which, given her perilous circumstances, could be described as brave.

The case against her was that she had acquired sums of money from Mr X (a businessman from Beckenham) by threatening to tell Mrs X that their friendly encounters took place between the sheets. The facts were, as you see, routine. What was unusual was that Maureen's twelve-year-old son Edmund, a solemn child wearing spectacles and a school blazer, was seated on a bench outside Court Number Two reading a paperback called *Sensational Trials*. Edmund, it seemed, was short of a minder and took an interest in crime.

"Mr X," I stood up to cross-examine Maureen's alleged victim, a thin-faced, anxious-looking individual with a bald patch and a habit of dabbing a slightly sweaty top lip with a folded handkerchief, "how long had your love affair with Maureen O'Keefe lasted?"

"We had known each other for four years."

"You could scarcely call it a love affair!" The voice of Mr Justice Graves blew down like a cold wind from the bench. "More a business arrangement."

"Whatever you call it, how much money did you give her over that period?"

"He has already told us, Mr Rumpole. Just under £4,000."

There were times when I would have loved to plant a heavy tombstone on old Graves to stop him interrupting.

"Four thousand?" I concentrated on the witness. "Under a thousand a year? Hardly enough to set her up with a yacht and a Jaguar, or even a small boutique."

"It was a little more than I could afford."

"But not more than any man might give as presents to his mistress?"

"Were they *presents*?" Graves made the word sound as though everything gift-wrapped and handed over at Christmas was the result of some kind of criminal conspiracy.

"I suppose you could call them that," Mr X conceded, to the obvious annoyance of the old Graveyard.

"And Maureen might have thought of them as presents?"

"I suppose she might."

"The sort of presents any man might give his girlfriend?"

"Perhaps."

"And, as we already know, you gave her this money in cheques. Wasn't that a little risky? I suppose your wife might see your bank statements?"

"She did. She rang the bank."

"What did you tell her?"

"I told her Miss O'Keefe was someone who did my part-time typing. She made further inquiries ...

"And found out you'd lied?"

"Yes."

"And was it your wife who suggested you must have been blackmailed and you should go to the police, hoping she'd get your money back?"

"It was my wife's idea, yes."

"You didn't want to bring this case, did you, Mr X?"

"No. It's been embarrassing."

"Embarrassing for you, certainly. And perhaps ruinous for the lady I have the honour to represent." I said this proudly, raising my arm in a salute towards Maureen and smiling for the benefit of the jury. "And tell me, Mr X," I turned the full power of the Rumpole searching look on the man. "Did Maureen ever mention your wife to you?"

"She said it would be a pity if my wife found out."

"Isn't that just the sort of thing any mistress might say to her lover? Without any idea of blackmail being involved at all?"

"I suppose that's possible."

"I suppose it is. And tell me this, Mr X, since you can shelter behind an anonymity denied to the lady put up in the dock for all the tabloids to scorn." (In fact there had been disappointingly little reference to *R. v. O'Keefe* in the papers.) "Were you truly grateful for what she did for you?"

"I suppose I was."

"And don't you suppose that she accepted this less than £1,000 per annum for always being ready and available whenever you happened to ring her up on the telephone?"

"I suppose that's possible, yes."

"And she never had blackmail in her mind at all?"

There was a pause. Mr X looked up to heaven, trying to avoid the disapproving gaze of Mrs X, large and fur-coated, who sat beside his solicitor.

Finally he dabbed his upper lip and said, "That's possible."

"Thank you, Mr X. That word 'possible' is all that is required of you!"

So I folded my gown about me and sat down. Mr Justice Graves gave me a stony look, as though I were the sole instigator of a blackmail plot and I should be immediately placed beside my client in the dock.

"Edmund wants to be like you, Mr Rumpole. He's got ambitions to be a brief." Maureen had told me that when the jury was sent out and before she was taken down to the cells to await their decision. "Poor little chap. He must have got tired of waiting. Would you see he gets a cup of something hot?"

So there I was, enduring the worst part of any trial, the long wait when there's nothing else to do, nothing else you can say to affect the result, and your client's fate is in the hands of the honest, attentive, or not so attentive, twelve. I was in the Old Bailey canteen with a solemn child for whom I had bought sweet tea and chocolate biscuits and whom I thought I had seen, at moments during his mother's trial, peep round the door of the court before an usher hustled him back to his seat outside.

As he kindly allowed me to light up a small cigar, Edmund said, "Mum says you did brilliantly for her in court, Mr Rumpole. You been at the job a long time, have you?"

"Sometimes it seems since the dawn of time."

"I bet you could have got that Dr Crippen off if you'd've been his brief. The one what chopped his wife up and buried her in the cellar."

"Dr Crippen was, I'm afraid, before my time."

"What would you have said, Mr Rumpole, if you had to stand up for that old doctor, like?" There was an eager glint behind Edmund's glasses.

"He didn't mean to kill her," I suggested. "He just gave her Hyoscine to keep her quiet at night. She was a great chatterer, you know. Drove him out of his mind. Well, she took too many sleeping pills and pegged out."

"Mr Rumpole! That's brilliant!" Edmund's admiration seemed genuine.

"Not my idea. Marshall Hall's. The greatest criminal barrister of all time."

"How'd you explain him cutting her up, like?"

"Panic, I suppose. But that's the most difficult part of the case."

"You'd get over it, Mr Rumpole. I bet you would. Mum said you handled the bloke what charged her just perfect. In your cross-examination."

"You know that expression?"

"Of course. It comes in my *Sensational Trials* book. As it does in Sir Edward Marshall Hall."

"Cross-examining," I explained to Edmund, "is not the art of examining crossly. I was polite to Mr X. I treated him like a friend. I led him gently by the hand up the garden path and dropped him in the compost heap. I'm sorry you missed it."

"I heard a bit. I got the door open a little."

This Edmund, I thought, was a lad who might go far in the law, whether in or out of the dock. But I thought I should direct his thoughts back to childhood.

"Christmas is coming, Edmund," I reminded him. "What're you hoping for?"

"Pterodactyl!" The boy had no doubt about it. "Extinct flying reptile of the Jurassic period. They got them electronically powered, so they're ever so realistic. I know that's what Mum's going to get me for Christmas."

I was by no means certain that his mum would be at liberty to go shopping, but I didn't tell Edmund that.

The jury were either unable to make up their minds or

had sent for tea. I wondered what would happen to Edmund if the news were to be bad and, in one insane moment, I tried to imagine the reaction of She Who Must Be Obeyed if I brought Edmund home to Froxbury Mansions for her to look after during a four-year sentence.

Happily this scene of high tragedy and matrimonial mayhem was avoided. Ten minutes later we were called back into court, the jury found Maureen O'Keefe "not guilty" and that was the verdict of them all.

She gave me a kiss and said, "Thanks for that, Mr Rumpole, darling."

Edmund said, "Brilliant! Better than Sir Edward Marshall Hall!" And they walked off together into the early sunset.

Christmas was coming nearer and, as the threat of the festive season approached, there was a nasty slump in business. Where had all the villains got to? Were they taking winter breaks in Florida or on the Costa del Crime? Had they gone into retirement and taken to buying their Christmas presents instead of nicking them in the usual manner? Had the season of goodwill come down on us with such a thump that pawnbrokers were leaving their doors unlocked and finding no takers?

Whatever the reason, my diary, apart from the odd indecency in Snaresbrook, was sadly empty and my mantelpiece held very few briefs indeed. I was even stumped by the crossword puzzle when there was a knock at my door and Henry, our clerk, put his head round and told me I had a visitor.

"Someone in trouble?" I asked hopefully.

"If he is, it's a matter for the juvenile court. Not much of a brief fee on that. I should imagine."

And with that he introduced young Edmund O'Keefe into my presence. He made himself comfortable in my client's armchair and said, "Thanks for letting me come and see you, Mr Rumpole. Mum said you'd probably be terribly busy, but the clerk said you was in, so she thought you might be so kind as to keep an eye on me while she goes out after the you-know-what."

"I'm afraid I don't know what."

"What we was talking about down at the Old Bailey. While the jury was out. We was talking about this extinct flying reptile."

"Edmund!" I was mildly reproving. "I may have expressed some criticism of our learned trial judge, but I'm sure I didn't go so far as to call him an extinct flying reptile!"

"No. You know what I mean, Mr Rumpole. The pterodactyl!"

"Oh, you're talking about our prosecuting counsel?"

"What I want for Christmas! I'm sure Mum's gone out to

buy it for me. But she thinks I can't guess what she's up to. She asked me to meet her in three-quarters of an hour at Oxford Circus station. I'll be going to the Tube soon, but if I could just sit here quietly, in the warm?"

"Yes, Edmund. Of course you can." So I took up my pen and tried the anagrams in the crossword and hoped that it looked as though I was working hard.

After a while Edmund offered me a curiously strong mint, which I accepted, and then he said, "Mum told me that quite often, during her trial I mean, you were really rude to the old judge. Is that a good idea? I mean, I want to know for when I'm a brief."

He was talking about the work which I had been dealing with, man and boy, for almost half a century, so I gave him the full benefit of my experience.

"Well, you see, Edmund. It's like this. If the judge is obviously on your side you flatter him, butter him up, say fawning things like 'as your Lordship, with his vast experience of these matters, knows so much better than I . . .' and it's in the bag. On the other hand," I warned young Edmund, "if the judge is completely fair and sums up straight down the line the jury are quite likely to convict. But if the judge is a real prosecution-minded bastard who's dead set on potting you . . ."

"What's 'potting,' Mr Rumpole?"

"Knocking your client into the pocket with a long cue. Dropping him into chokey."

"Like Mr Justice Graves?"

"You're absolutely right. Just like old Graveyard. Then you taunt him, irritate him, play him like a matador plays a bull. Get him to behave so that the jury takes against him and your client gets off."

"Is that how you got my mum off?" Edmund asked.

"Not altogether. I got her off by my brilliant cross-examination of Mr X. After that, the jury couldn't be sure of anything." There was a silence, during which Edmund absorbed this wisdom and gave me another mint. Then he said, "What was the real truth about the bloodstains in the Penge Bungalow case, Mr Rumpole?"

"The Penge Bungalow! How on earth do you know about that?"

"It's in my book of sensational trials."

"Is it really?" My dark afternoon was lit up by the golden glow of an old triumph. "I did that case when I was a young white-wig. Alone and without a leader. I won it by my extensive knowledge of bloodstains. Might I have a look at that book of yours?"

"I'll lend it to you, Mr Rumpole. I'll give you *Sensational Trials* as soon as I've finished with it. But while we're talking about these famous murders ... did Alma Rattenbury know her boyfriend was planning to do her husband in with a croquet mallet, do you think?"

I gave him my view, which was that Mrs Rattenbury was entirely innocent of any crime worse than adultery with a boy scout, and we went on to other cases. We considered whether the Brides in the Bath murderer would ever have been convicted if he hadn't gone into the witness box and made a bad impression on the jury.

What had been an achingly boring afternoon became quite pleasant, until Edmund looked at the clock on my naked mantelpiece and discovered he had only ten minutes to be at Oxford Circus Tube to meet his mother. He asked the way to Temple Station, but I told the lad, who seemed likely to have a successful career in murder opening before him, that I would take him in a taxi and then go on to the so-called "Mansion Flat" in the Gloucester Road. It seemed a small price to pay for learning that I was in a Sensational Trial.

When we got to Oxford Circus Tube it was, of course, crowded, but we saw neither hide nor hair of Maureen O'Keefe. We stood, first on one side, then on another in the way of passing crowds of busy men with briefcases and girls with bright shopping bags, but that blonde head, darker at the roots, never bobbed on the surface of humanity.

.   .   .

My encouraging phrases—"She'll be here in a minute"; "Let's just wait and she's bound to see us"; "No, Edmund, I'm sure she hasn't forgotten you"—began to lack conviction.

In vain I tried to interest him in more sensational murders. I went through the Supermarket Strangulation, the Hampstead Cinema Stabbing, the Death at The Circus and the mysterious affair of the body found in the deep freezer of a Thai restaurant, but I could see that the boy's attention was wandering. He had got to that desperate stage of human anxiety when even the juiciest murder can't take your mind off your troubles.

Edmund was beginning, I felt, to fear that his mother was never coming and had run out on him, and the same thought was occurring to me. Had Maureen upped sticks and returned to Ireland? Had she been arrested for some other offence and detained without bail? Had she planned to leave her offspring with me, where he would be sure of a good home and a training in the finer points of the criminal law? I felt the cold hand of fear grip me as I thought, once more, of explaining to Hilda that our little family had been suddenly enlarged.

And then Claude Erskine-Brown, the opera-loving wine buff and hopeless advocate from our chambers, arose from the murky depths, no doubt in search of Mrs Justice Erskine-Brown.

"No, Erskine-Brown. It is not my grandson."

"Your nephew, then?"

"Not my nephew either."

"Well, who is it?"

"A young friend of mine."

"A friend?" Erskine-Brown looked at me with deep suspicion. "What sort of friend?"

"The sort that knows a bit about murder. Which is more than can be said of you, Claude. I'd like you to meet . . ."

Before I could effect the introduction, a sudden thought had struck Edmund and cheered him up considerably. He gave a loud cry of "I know what's happened to my mum! She must have gone off to buy the pterodactyl!" and he vanished into the milling, moving surge of shoppers and was carried away by them, out of my sight, like a toy boat disappearing on a choppy sea. Now I feared that Maureen hadn't ditched him, and that I would eventually have to explain to a weeping mother that I had lost her child in Oxford Street. I set off, no doubt foolishly, in hot pursuit.

It was a nightmare. I was being pushed and shoved battling against bodies carrying shopping bags and huge parcels or pushing baskets on wheels. I was outstared by pale, obsessed, rebuking faces, shouted at to "Mind where you're going!" or blankly ignored by those who had been taken over by shopping as though it were some hallucinatory drug.

Above us the lights, the illuminated patterns, lit-up toys,

hung like phantom bridges under which we scurried. Pop music, blaring from record shops, battered my ears. Men in anoraks, sidling up, tried to sell me video games at give-away prices. Old women, bundled into doorways, stretched their arms out towards me and begged for "change." I passed an "Erotic Gear" store, with a window of black leather and chains, from which the strains of "Silent Night" were emerging. I called out for "Edmund!" once or twice, but it was like shouting into a hurricane.

And then I saw him. He was walking fast, trying to keep up with a man in a dark suit who had a possessive arm around his shoulder. Sadly, we live in an age when we're afraid that no twelve-year-old can walk through a crowd unattended without risk of kidnapping, sexual assault or even death. With this in mind I decided to give chase.

In my imagination there was something sinister about the dark-suited figure with his protective arm about Edmund's shoulder. Might he not be a prowling paedophile who'd made a catch? I panted. I broke, at moments, into a sort of shambling trot. Unfit for such exercise by reason of fried slices and small cigars, I ended up coughing. My quarry was sometimes visible, sometimes hidden by the crowd. They crossed roads just as the traffic lights were changing, and then I had to put on another turn of speed. For a good five minutes I seemed to have lost them.

And then I saw them turn away from the crowds, off Oxford Street and up Rathbone Place into northern Soho. I trotted shambolically after them. They were fifty yards ahead of me, going past the lit restaurants in Charlotte Street. Then they went into Fitzroy Street and the lights changed. I was prevented from crossing by a swerving motorbike and hooting taxis. But I saw them in the doorway of a pale house with peeling stucco. The sinister man put a finger to the bell and before I had crossed the road I saw the door open and he and Edmund had vanished inside.

When I got to the door it was locked again. There was a vertical line of bell pushes with names like "Trixie," "Yo–Yo," "Georgie" and "Lalique." There was no "Maureen." I pressed "Yo-Yo" for luck and an old, tired voice said, "Come on up, dear." The door clicked and let me in.

I went up a dirty stairway and smelled face powder and disinfectant and take-away food. Then I heard the voice of a young boy. "Thank you very much! It's exactly what I wanted!"

I opened the door which separated me from the cry of delight. I was in a room with a gas fire, a candlewick bedspread, the smell of cheap scent and a small, lit-up Christmas tree. Maureen and Mr X were kneeling on each side of Edmund, like a picture of the Christmas Family. On the floor, squawking and flashing, was the pterodactyl Mr X had no doubt given Edmund early, because he wouldn't be able to get away to visit them on Christmas Day.

It was then I realized that I hadn't forced admissions out of Mr X with the brilliance of my cross-examination at the trial. Mr X had simply given his case away for Christmas.

Rumpole and the Old Familiar Faces

In the varied ups and downs, the thrills and spills in the life of an Old Bailey hack, one thing stands as stone. Your ex-customers will never want to see you again. Even if you've steered them through the rocks of the prosecution case and brought them out to the calm waters of a not guilty verdict, they won't plan further meetings, host reunion dinners, or even send you a card on your birthday. If they catch a glimpse of you on the Underground, or across a crowded wine bar, they will bury their faces in their newspapers or look studiously in the opposite direction. This is understandable. Days in court probably represent a period of time they'd rather forget and, as a rule, I'm not especially keen to renew an old acquaintance when a face I once saw in the Old Bailey dock reappears at a "Scales of Justice" dinner or at the Inns of Court garden party. Reminiscences of the past are best avoided, and what is required is a quick look and a quiet turn away. There have been times, however, when recognizing a face seen in trouble has greatly assisted me in the solution of some legal problem and carried me to triumph in a difficult case. Such occasions have been rare but, like number thirteen buses, two of them turned up in short order around a Christmas which I remember as being one of the oddest, but certainly the most rewarding, I ever spent.

"A traditional British pantomime. There's nothing to beat it!"

"You go to the pantomime, Rumpole?" Claude asked with unexpected interest.

"I did when I was a boy. It made a lasting impression on me."

"Pantomime?" The American judge who was our fellow guest around the Erskine-Brown dinner table was clearly a stranger to such delights. "Is that some kind of mime show? Lots of feeling imaginary walls and no one saying anything?"

"Not at all. You take some good old story, like *Robin Hood* . . ."

"Robin Hood's the star?"

"Well, yes. He's played by some strapping girl who slaps her thighs and says lines like, 'Cheer up, Babes in the Wood, Robin's not far away.'"

"You mean there's cross-dressing?" The American visitor was puzzled.

"Well, if you want to call it that. And Robin's mother is played by a red-nosed comic."

"A female comic?"

"No. A male one."

"That sounds interesting," he said in a tone that suggested he had the wrong idea. "We have clubs for that sort of thing in Pittsburgh."

"It's not what you're thinking," I assured him. "The dame's a comic character who gets the audience singing."

"Singing?"

"The words come down on a sort of giant song sheet," I explained, "and she, who is really a he, gets the audience to sing along."

Emboldened by Erskine-Brown's claret (smoother on the tongue but with less of a kick than Château Thames Embankment), I broke into a stanza of the song I was introduced to by Robin Hood's masculine mother.

I may be just a nipper,
But I've always loved a kipper ...
And so does my loving wife.
If you've got a girl, just slip her
A loving golden kipper
And she'll be yours for life.

"Is that all?" The transatlantic judge still seemed puzzled.

"All I can remember."

"I think you're wrong, Mr Rumpole."

"What?"

"I think you're wrong and those lines do indeed have some significance along the lines I suggested." And the judge fell silent, contemplating the unusual acts suggested.

"I see they're doing *Aladdin* at the Tufnell Park Empire. Do you think the twins might enjoy it, Rumpole?"

The speaker was Mrs Justice Erskine-Brown (Phillida Trant as she was in happier days when I called her the Portia of our chambers), still possessed of a beauty that would break the hearts of the toughest prosecutors and make old lags swoon with lust even as she passed a stiff custodial sentence. The twins she spoke of were Tristan and Isolde, so named by her opera-loving husband Claude, who was now bending Hilda's ear on the subject of Covent Garden's latest *Ring* cycle.

"I think the twins would adore it. Just the thing to cure the Wagnerian death wish and bring them into a world of sanity."

"Sanity?" The visiting judge sounded doubtful. "With old guys dressed up as mothers?"

"I promise you, they'll love every minute of it." And then I made another promise that sounded rash even as I spoke the words. "I know I would. I'll take them myself."

"Thank you, Rumpole." Phillida spoke in her gentlest judicial voice, but I knew my fate was sealed. "We'll keep you to that."

"It'll have to be after Christmas," Hilda said. "We've been invited up to Norfolk for the holiday."

"As she said the word 'Norfolk' a cold, sweeping wind seemed to cut through the central heating of the Erskine-Browns' Islington dining room and I felt a warning shiver.

I have no rooted objection to Christmas Day, but I must say it's an occasion when time tends to hang particularly heavily on the hands. From the early morning alarm call of carols piping on Radio Four to the closing headlines and a restless, liverish sleep, the day can seem as long as a fraud on the Post Office tried before Mr Injustice Graves.

It takes less than no time for me to unwrap the tie which I will seldom wear, and for Hilda to receive the annual bottle of lavender water which she lays down rather than puts to immediate use. The highlights after that are the Queen's speech, when I lay bets with myself as to whether Hilda will stand to attention when the television plays the National Anthem, and the thawed-out Safeway bird followed by port (an annual gift from my faithful solicitor Bonny Bernard) and pudding. I suppose what I have against Christmas Day is that the courts are all shut and no one is being tried for anything.

That Christmas, Hilda had decided on a complete change of routine. She announced it in a circuitous fashion by saying, one late November evening, "I was at school with Poppy Longstaff."

"What's that got to do with it?" I knew the answer to this question, of course. Hilda's old school has this in common with polar expeditions, natural disasters and the last war; those who have lived through it are bound together for life and can always call on each other for mutual assistance.

"Poppy's Eric is Rector of Coldsands. And for some reason or other he seems to want to meet you, Rumpole."

"Meet me?"

"That's what she said."

"So does that mean I have to spend Christmas in the Arctic Circle and miss our festivities?"

"It's not the Arctic Circle. It's Norfolk, Rumpole. And our festivities aren't all that festive. So, yes. You have to go." It was a judgement for which there was no possible appeal.

. . .

My first impression of Coldsands was a gaunt church tower, presumably of great age, pointing an accusing finger to heaven from a cluster of houses on the edge of a sullen, gun-metal sea. My second was one of intense cold. As soon as we got out of the taxi, we were slapped around the face by a wind which must have started in freezing Siberia and gained nothing in the way of warmth on its journey across the plains of Europe.

"In the bleak midwinter / Frosty winds made moan . . ." wrote that sad old darling Christina Rossetti. Frosty winds made considerable moan round the rectory at Coldsands, owing to the doors that stopped about an inch short of the stone floors and the windows which never shut properly, causing the curtains to billow like the sails of a ship at sea.

We were greeted cheerfully by Poppy. Hilda's friend had one of those round, childishly pretty faces often seen on seriously fat women. She seemed to keep going on incessant cups of hot, sweet tea and a number of cardigans. If she moved like an enormous tent, her husband Eric was a slender wraith of a man with a high aquiline nose, two flapping wings of grey hair on each side of his face and a vague air of perpetual anxiety broken, now and then, by high and unexpected laughter. He made cruciform gestures, as though remembering the rubric "spectacles, testicles, wallet and watch" and forgetting where these important articles were kept.

"Eric," his wife explained, "is having terrible trouble with the church tower."

"Oh, dear." Hilda shot me a look of stern disapproval, which I knew meant that it would be more polite if I abandoned my overcoat while tea was being served. "How worrying for you, Eric."

The Revd Eric went into a long, excited and high-pitched speech. The gist of it was that the tower, although of rare beauty, had not been much restored since the Saxons built it and the Normans added the finishing touches. Fifty thousand pounds was needed for essential repairs, and the thermometer, erected outside the church for the appeal, was stuck at one hundred and twenty pounds—the proceeds from an emergency jumble sale.

"You particularly wanted Horace to come this Christmas?" Hilda asked the Man of God with the air of someone anxious to solve a baffling mystery. "I wonder why that was?"

"Yes. I wonder!" Eric looked startled. "I wonder why on earth I wanted to ask Horace. I don't believe he's got fifty thousand smackers in his back pocket!" At this, he shook with laughter.

"There," I told him, "your lack of faith is entirely justified."

I wasn't exactly enjoying Coldsands Rectory, so I was a little miffed that the Reverend couldn't remember why he'd asked me there in the first place.

"We had hoped that Donald Compton would help us out," Poppy told us. "I mean, he wouldn't notice fifty thousand. But he took exception to what Eric said at the Remembrance Day service."

"Armistice Day in the village." Eric's grey wings of hair trembled as he nodded in delighted affirmation. "And I prayed for dead German soldiers. It seemed only fair."

"Fair perhaps, darling. But hardly tactful," his wife told him. "Donald Compton thought it was distinctly unpatriotic. He's bought the Old Manor House," she explained to Hilda. From then on the conversation turned exclusively to this Compton and was carried on in the tones of awe and muted wonder with which people always talk about the very rich. Compton, it seemed, after a difficult start in England, had gone to Canada where, during a ten-year stay, he had laid the foundations of his fortune. His much younger wife was quite charming, probably Canadian, and not in the least stand-offish. He had built the village hall, the cricket pavilion, and a tennis court for the school. Only Eric's unfortunate sympathy for the German dead had caused Compton's bounty to stop short at the church tower.

"I've done hours of hard knee-work," the rector told us,

"begging the Lord to soften Mr Compton's heart towards our tower. No result so far, I fear."

Apart from this one lapse, the charming Donald Compton seemed to be the perfect English squire and country gent. I would see him in church on Christmas morning, and we had also been invited for drinks before lunch at the manor. The Reverend Eric and the smiling Poppy made it sound as though the Pope and the Archbishop of Canterbury would be out with the carol singers and we'd been invited to drop in for high tea at Windsor Castle. I prayed for a yule log blazing at the manor so that I could, in the true spirit of Christmas, thaw out gradually.

"Now, as a sign of Christmas fellowship, will you all stand and shake hands with those in front of and behind you?" Eric, in full canonicals, standing on the steps in front of the altar, made this suggestion as though he had just thought of the idea. I stood reluctantly. I had found myself a place in the church near a huge, friendly, gently humming, occasionally belching radiator and I was clinging to it and stroking it as though it were a newfound mistress (not that I have much experience of new- or even old-found mistresses). The man who turned to me from the front row seemed to be equally reluctant. He was, as Hilda had pointed out excitedly, the great Donald Compton in person—a man of middle height with silver hair, dressed in a tweed suit, and with a tan which it must have been expensive to preserve during winter. He had soft brown eyes which looked away from me almost at once as, with a touch of dry fingers, he was gone and I was left, for the rest of the service, with no more than a well-tailored back and the sound of an uncertain tenor voice joining in the hymns.

I turned to the row behind to shake hands with an elderly woman who had madness in her eyes and whispered conspiratorially to me, "You cold, dear? Like to borrow my gloves? We're used to a bit of chill weather round these parts." I declined politely and went back to hugging the radiator, and as I did so a sort of happiness stole over me. To start with, the church was beautiful, with a high timbered roof and walls of weathered stone, peppered with marble tributes to dead inhabitants of the manor. It was decorated with holly and mistletoe. A tree glowed and there were candles over a crib. I thought how many generations of Coldsands villagers, their eyes bright and faces flushed with the wind, had belted out these hymns. I also thought how depressed the great Donald Compton—who had put on little gold half-glasses to read the prophecy from Isaiah: "For unto us a child is born, unto us a son is given: and the government shall be upon his shoulder: and his name shall be called Wonderful"—would feel if Jesus' instruction to sell all and give it to the poor should ever be taken literally.

And then I wondered why it was that, as he had touched my fingers and turned away, I had felt that I had lived through that precise moment before.

There was, as it turned out, a huge log fire crackling at the manor, throwing a dancing light on the marble floor of the circular entrance hall with its great staircase leading up into private shadows. The cream of Coldsands was being entertained with champagne and canapés by the new Lord of the Manor. The decibels rose as the champagne went down and the little group began to sound like an army of tourists in the Sistine Chapel—noisy, excited and wonderstruck.

"They must all be his ancestors." Hilda was looking at the pictures on the walls and, in particular, at a general in a scarlet coat, on a horse prancing at the front of some distant battle.

My mouth was full of cream cheese enveloped in smoked salmon. I swallowed it and said, "Oh, I shouldn't think so. After all, he only bought the house recently."

"But I expect he brought his family portraits here from somewhere else."

"You mean, he had them under the bed in his old bachelor flat in Wimbledon and now he's hung them round an acre or two of walls?"

"Do try and be serious, Rumpole. You're not nearly as funny as you think you are. Just look at the family resemblance. I'm absolutely certain that all of these are old Comptons." And it was when she said this that I remembered everything perfectly clearly.

He was with his wife. She was wearing a black velvet dress and had long, golden hair that sparkled in the firelight. They were talking to a bald, pink-faced man and his short and dumpy wife, and they were all laughing. Compton's laughter stopped as he saw me coming towards him. He said, "I don't think we've met."

"Yes," I replied. "We shook hands briefly in church this morning. My name's Rumpole and I'm staying with the Longstaffs. But didn't we meet somewhere else?"

"Good old Eric! We have our differences, of course, but he's a saintly man. This is my wife Lorelei, and Colonel and Maudy Jacobs. I expect you'd like to see the library, wouldn't you, Rumpole? I'm sure you're interested in ancient history. Will you all excuse us?"

It was two words from Hilda that had done it—"old" and "Compton." I knew then what I should have remembered when we had touched hands in the pews, that Old Compton is a street in Soho, and that this was perhaps why Riccardo (known as Dicko) Perducci had adopted the name. I had received that very same handshake—a slight touch and a quick turn away—when I had said goodbye to him in the cells under the Old Bailey and left him to start seven years for blackmail. The trial had ended, I now remembered, just before a long-distant Christmas.

The Perducci territory had been, in those days, not rolling Norfolk acres but a number of Soho strip clubs and clip joints. Girls would stand in front of these last-named resorts and lure the lonely, the desperate and the unwary in. Sometimes they would escape after paying twenty pounds for a watery cocktail. Unlucky, affluent and important customers might get even more, carefully recorded by microphones and cameras to produce material which was used for systematic and highly profitable blackmail. The victim in Dicko's case was an obscure and not much loved circuit judge, so it was regarded as particularly serious by the prosecuting authority.

When I mitigated for Dicko, I stressed the lack of direct evidence against him. He was a shadowy figure who kept himself well in the background and was known as a legend rather than a familiar face around Soho. "That only shows what a big wheel he is," Judge Bullingham, who was unfortunately trying the case, bellowed unsympathetically. In desperation I tried the Christmas approach on him. "Crimes forgiven, sins remitted, mercy triumphant, such was the message of the story that began in Bethlehem," I told the court, at which the Mad Bull snorted that, as far as he could remember, that story had ended in a criminal trial and a stiff sentence for at least one thief.

"I suppose something like this was going to happen sooner or later." We were standing in the library in front of a comforting fire, among leather-bound books which I strongly suspected had been bought by the yard. The new, like the old, Dicko was soft-eyed, quietly spoken, almost unnaturally calm—the perfect man behind the scenes of a blackmailing operation or a country estate.

"Not necessarily," I told him. "It's just that my wife has many old school friends and Poppy Longstaff is one of them. Well now, you seem to have done pretty well for yourself. Solid citizens still misconducting themselves around Old Compton Street, are they?"

"I wouldn't know. I gave all that up and went into the property business."

"Really? Where did you do that? Canada?"

"I never saw Canada." He shook his head. "Garwick Prison. Up-and-coming area in the Home Counties. The screws there were ready and willing to do the deals on the outside. I paid them embarrassingly small commissions."

"How long were you there?"

"Four years. By the time I came out I'd got my first million."

"Well, then, I did you a good turn, losing your case. A bit of luck His Honour Judge Bullingham didn't believe in the remission of sins."

"You think I got what I deserved?"

I stretched my hands to the fire. I could hear the cocktail chatter from the marble hall of the eighteenth-century manor. "Use every man after his desert, and who should 'scape whipping?" I quoted *Hamlet* at him.

"Then I can trust you, Rumpole? The Lord Chancellor's going to put me on the local bench."

"The Lord Chancellor lives in a world of his own."

"You don't think I'd do well as a magistrate?"

"I suppose you'd speak from personal experience of crime. And have some respect for the quality of mercy."

"I've got no time for that, Rumpole." His voice became quieter but harder. The brown eyes lost their softness. That, I thought, was how he must have looked when one of his clip joint girls was caught with the punters' cash stuffed in her tights. "It's about time we cracked down on crime. Well, now, I can trust you not to go out there and spread the word about the last time we met?"

"That depends."

"On what?"

"How well you have understood the Christmas message."

"Which is?"

"Perhaps, generosity."

"I see. So you want your bung?"

"Oh, not me, Dicko. I've been paid, inadequately, by Legal Aid. But there's an impoverished church tower in urgent need of resuscitation."

"That Eric Longstaff, our rector—he's not a patriot!"

"And are you?"

"I do a good deal of work locally for the British Legion."

"And, I'm sure, next Poppy Day they'll appreciate what you've done for the church tower."

He looked at me for a long minute in silence, and I thought that if this scene had been taking place in a back room in Soho there might, quite soon, have been the flash of a knife. Instead, his hand went to an inside pocket and produced nothing more lethal than a chequebook.

"While you're in a giving mood," I said, "the rectory's in desperate need of central heating."

"This is bloody blackmail!" Dicko Perducci, now known as Donald Compton, said.

"Well," I told him, "you should know."

Christmas was over. The year turned, stirred itself and opened its eyes on a bleak January. Crimes were committed, arrests were made and the courtrooms were filled, once again, with the sounds of argument. I went down to the Old Bailey on a trifling matter of fixing the date of a trial before Mrs Justice Erskine-Brown. As I was leaving, the usher came and told me that the judge wanted to see me in her private room on a matter of urgency.

Such summonses always fill me with apprehension and a vague feeling of guilt. What had I done? Got the date of the trial hopelessly muddled? Addressed the Court with my trousers carelessly unzipped? I was relieved when the learned Phillida greeted me warmly and even offered me a glass of sherry, poured from her own personal decanter. "It was so kind of you to offer, Rumpole," she said unexpectedly.

"Offer what?" I was puzzled.

"You told us how much you adored the traditional British pantomime."

"So I did." For a happy moment I imagined Her Ladyship as Principal Boy, her shapely legs encased in black tights, her neat little wig slightly askew, slapping her thigh and calling out, in bell-like tones, "Cheer up, Rumpole, Portia's not far away."

"The twins are looking forward to it enormously."

"Looking forward to what?"

"*Aladdin* at the Tufnell Park Empire. I've got tickets for the nineteenth of January. You do remember promising to take them, don't you?"

"Well, of course." What else might I have said after the fifth glass of Erskine-Brown St Emilion? "I'd love to be of the party. And will old Claude be buying us a dinner afterwards?"

"I really don't think you should go around calling people 'old,' Rumpole." Phillida now looked miffed, and I downed the sherry before she took it into her head to deprive me of it. "Claude's got us tickets for Pavarotti—*L'Elisir d'Amore*. You might buy the children a burger after the show. Oh, and it's not far from us on the Tube. It really was sweet of you to invite them." At which she smiled at me and refilled my glass in a way which made it clear she was not prepared to hear further argument.

It all turned out better than I could have hoped. Tristan and Isolde, unlike their Wagnerian namesakes, were cheerful, reasonably polite and only seemed anxious to disassociate themselves, as far as possible, from the old fart who was escorting them. At every available opportunity they would touch me for cash and then scamper off to buy ice cream, chocolates, sandwiches or Sprite. I was left in reasonable peace to enjoy the performance.

And enjoy it I did. Aladdin was a personable young woman with an upturned nose, a voice which could have been used to wake up patients coming round from their anaesthesia and memorable thighs. Uncle Abanazer was played, Isolde told me, by an actor who portrayed a social worker with domestic problems in a long-running television series. Wishy and Washy did sing to electric guitars (deafeningly amplified) but Widow Twankey, played by a certain Jim Diamond, was all a dame should be—a nimble little Cockney, fitted up with a sizeable false bosom, a flaming red wig, sweeping eyelashes and scarlet lips. Never have I heard the immortal line "Where's that naughty boy Aladdin got to?" better delivered. I joined in loudly (Tristan and Isolde sat silent and embarrassed) when the Widow and Aladdin conducted us in the singing of "Please Don't Pinch My Tomatoes." It was, in fact and in fairness, all a traditional pantomime should be, and yet I had a vague feeling that something was wrong, that an element was missing. But, as the cast came down a white staircase in glittering costumes to enthusiastic applause, it seemed the sort of pantomime I'd grown up with and which Tristan and Isolde should be content to inherit.

After so much excitement I felt in need of a stiff brandy and soda, but the eatery the children had selected for their evening's entertainment had apparently gone teetotal and alcohol was not on the menu. Once they were confronted by their mammoth burgers and fries I made my excuses, said I'd be back in a moment and slipped into a nearby pub which was, I noticed, opposite the stage door of the Empire.

As the life-giving draught was being poured I found myself standing next to Washy and Uncle Abanazer, now out of costume, who were discussing Jim the Dame. "Very unfriendly tonight," Washy said. "Locked himself in his dressing room before the show and wouldn't join us for a drink."

"Perhaps he's had a bust-up with Molly?"

"Unlikely. Molly and Jim never have a cross word."

"Lucky she's never found out he's been polishing Aladdin's wonderful lamp," Abanazer said, and they both laughed.

As I asked the girl behind the bar to refill my glass, in which the tide had sunk to a dangerous low, I heard them laugh again about the Widow Twankey's voluminous bosom. "Strapped-on polystyrene," Abanazer was saying. "Almost bruises me when I dance with her. Funny thing, tonight it was quite soft."

"Perhaps she borrowed one from a blow-up woman?" Washy was laughing as I gulped my brandy and legged it back to the hamburgers. In the dark passage outside the stage door I saw a small, nimble figure in hurried retreat— Jim Diamond, who for some reason hadn't wanted to join the boys at the bar.

After I had restored the children to the Erskine-Browns' au pair I sat in the Tube on my way back to Gloucester Road and read the programme. Jim Diamond, it seemed, had started his life in industry before taking up show business. He had a busy career in clubs and turned down appearances on television. "I only enjoy the living show," Jim says. "I want to have the audience where I can see them." His photograph, without the exaggerated female make-up, showed a pale, thin-nosed, in some way disagreeable little man with a lip curled either in scorn or triumph. I wondered how such an unfriendly-looking character could become an ebullient and warm-hearted widow. Stripped of his make-up, there was something about this comic's unsmiling face which brought back memories of another meeting in totally different circumstances. It was the second time within a few weeks that I had found an old familiar face cast in a new and unexpected part.

The memory I couldn't quite grasp preyed on my mind until I was tucked up in bed. Then, as Hilda's latest historical romance dropped from her weary fingers and she turned her back on me and switched out the light, I saw the face again quite clearly but in a different setting. Not Diamond. Sparker? No, Sparksman. A logical progression. Widow Twankey had been played by Harry Sparksman, a man who had trained as a professional entertainer, if my memory was correct, not in clubs, but in Her Majesty's prisons. It was, it seemed, an interesting career change, but I thought no more of it at the time and once satisfied with my identification I fell asleep.

"The boy couldn't have done it, Mr Rumpole. Not a complicated bloody great job to that extent. His only way of getting at a safe was to dig it out of the wall and remove it bodily. He did that in a Barkingside boutique and what he found in it hardly covered the petrol. Young Denis couldn't have got into the Croydon supermarket peter. No one in our family could have."

Uncle Fred, the experienced and cautious head of the Timson clan, had no regard for the safe-breaking talents of Denis, his nephew, and, on the whole, an unskilled recruit in the Timson enterprise. The Croydon supermarket job had been highly complicated and expertly carried out and had yielded, for its perpetrators, thousands of pounds. Peanuts Molloy was arrested as one of the lookouts after falling and twisting an ankle when chased by a night watchman during the getaway. He said he didn't know any of the skilled operators who had engaged him except Denis Timson who, he alleged, was in general charge of the operation. Denis alone, he said, had silenced the burglar alarm and deftly penetrated the lock on the safe with an oxyacetylene blowtorch.

It has to be remembered, though, that the clan Molloy had been sworn enemies of the Timson family from time immemorial. Peanuts' story sounded implausible when I met Denis Timson in the Brixton Prison interview room. A puzzled twenty-five-year-old with a shaven head and a poor attempt at a moustache, he seemed more upset by his Uncle Fred's low opinion of him than the danger of a conviction and subsequent prolonged absence from the family.

Denis's case was to come up for committal at the South London Magistrates' Court before "Skimpy" Simpson, whose lack of success at the Bar had driven him to a job as a stipendiary beak. His nickname had been earned by the fact that he had not, within living memory, been known to splash out on a round of drinks at Pommeroy's Wine Bar.

In the usual course of events, there is no future in fighting proceedings which are only there to commit the customer to trial. I had resolved to attend solely to pour a little well-deserved contempt on the testimony of Peanuts Molloy. As I started to prepare the case, I made a note of the date of the Croydon supermarket break-in. As soon as I had done so, I consulted my diary. I turned the virgin pages, as yet unstained by notes of trials, ideas for cross-examinations, splodges of tea, or spilled glasses of Pommeroy's Very Ordinary. It was as I had thought. While some virtuoso had been at work on the Croydon safe, I had been enjoying *Aladdin* in the company of Tristan and Isolde.

"Detective Inspector Grimble, would you agree that whoever blew the safe in the Croydon supermarket did an extraordinarily skilful job?"

"Mr Rumpole, are we meant to congratulate your client on his professional skill?"

God moves in mysterious ways, and it wasn't Skimpy Simpson's fault that he was born with thin lips and a voice which sounded like the rusty hinge of a rusty gate swinging in the wind. I decided to ignore him and concentrate on a friendly chat with DI Grimble, a large, comfortable, ginger-haired officer. We had both lived, over the years, with the clan Timson and their misdoings. He was known to them as a decent and fair-minded cop, as disapproving of the younger, Panda-racing, evidence-massaging intake to the force as they were of the lack of discretion and criminal skills which marked the younger Timsons.

"I mean, the thieves were well informed. They knew that there would be a week's money in the safe."

"They knew that, yes."

"And wasn't there a complex burglar alarm system? You couldn't put it out of action simply by cutting wires, could you?"

"Cutting the wires would have set it off."

"So putting the burglar alarm out of action would have required special skills?"

"It would have done."

"Putting it out of action also stopped a clock in the office. So we know that occurred at 8.45?"

"We know that. Yes."

"And at 9.20 young Molloy was caught as he fell while running to a getaway car."

"That is so."

"So this heavy safe was burned open in a little over half an hour?"

"I fail to see the relevance of this, Mr Rumpole." Skimpy was getting restless.

"I'm sure the officer does. That shows a very high degree of technical skill, doesn't it, Detective Inspector?"

"I'd agree with that."

"Exercised by a highly experienced peterman?"

"Who is this Mr Peterman?" Skimpy was puzzled. "We haven't heard of him before."

"Not *Mr* Peterman." I marvelled at the ignorance of the basic facts of life displayed by the magistrate. "A man expert at blowing safes, known to the trade as a 'peter,'" I told him and turned back to DI Grimble. "So we're agreed that this was a highly expert piece of work?"

"It must have been done by someone who knew his job pretty well. Yes."

"Denis Timson's record shows convictions for shoplifting, bag-snatching and stealing a radio from an unlocked car. In all of these simple enterprises, he managed to get caught."

"Your client's criminal record!" Skimpy looked happy for the first time. "You're allowing that to go into evidence, are you, Mr Rumpole?"

"Certainly, sir." I explained the obvious point. "Because there's absolutely no indication that he was capable of blowing a safe in record time, or silencing a complicated burglar alarm, is there, Detective Inspector?"

"No. There's nothing to show anything like that in his record . . ."

"Mr Rumpole." Skimpy was looking at the clock; was he in danger of missing his usual train back home to Haywards Heath? "Where's all this heading?"

"Back a good many years," I told him, "to the Sweet-Home Building Society job at Carshalton, when Harry Sparksman blew a safe so quietly that even the dogs slept through it."

"You were in on that case, weren't you, Mr Rumpole?" Inspector Grimble was pleased to remember. "Sparksman got five years."

"Not one of your great successes." Skimpy was also delighted. "Perhaps you wasted the court's time with unneces-sary questions. Have you anything else to ask this officer?"

"Not till the Old Bailey, Sir. I may have thought of a few more by then." With great satisfaction, Skimpy committed Denis Timson, a minor villain who would have had diffi-culty changing a fuse, let alone blowing a safe, for trial at the Central Criminal Court.

"Funny you mentioned Harry Sparksman. Do you know, the same thought occurred to me. An expert like him could've done that job in the time."

"Great minds think alike," I assured DI Grimble. We were washing away the memory of an hour or two before Skimpy with two pints of nourishing stout in the pub op-posite the beak's Court. "You know Harry took up a new career?" I needn't have asked the question. DI Grimble had a groupie's encyclopaedic knowledge of the criminal stars.

"Oh, yes. Now a comic called Jim Diamond. Got up a concert party in the nick. Apparently gave him a taste for show business."

"I did hear," I took Grimble into my confidence, "that he made a comeback for the Croydon job." It had been a throwaway line from Uncle Fred Timson—"I heard talk they got Harry back out of retirement"—but it was a thought worth examining.

"I heard the same. So we did a bit of checking. But Sparksman, known as Diamond, has got a cast-iron alibi."

"Are you sure?"

"At the time when the Croydon job was done, he was performing in a pantomime. On stage nearly all the evening, it seems, playing the Dame."

"*Aladdin*," I said, "at the Tufnell Park Empire. It might just be worth your while to go into that alibi a little more thoroughly. I'd suggest you have a private word with Mrs Molly Diamond. It's just possible she may have noticed his attraction to Aladdin's lamp."

"Now then, Mr Rumpole." Grimble was wiping the froth from his lips with a neatly folded handkerchief. "You mustn't tell me how to do my job."

"I'm only trying to serve," I managed to look pained, "the interests of justice!"

"You mean, the interests of your client?"

"Sometimes they're the same thing," I told him, but I had to admit it wasn't often.

As it happened, the truth emerged without Detective Inspector Grimble having to do much of a job. Harry had, in fact, fallen victim to a tip-tilted nose and memorable thighs; he'd left home and moved into Aladdin's Kensal Rise flat. Molly, taking a terrible revenge, blew his alibi wide open.

She had watched many rehearsals and knew every word, every gag, every nudge, wink and shrill complaint of the Dame's part. She had played it to perfection to give her husband an alibi while he went back to his old job in Croydon. It all went perfectly, even though Uncle Abanazer, dancing with her, had felt an unexpected softness.

I had known, instinctively, that something was very wrong. It had, however, taken some time for me to realize what I had really seen that night at the Tufnell Park Empire. It was nothing less than an outrage to a Great British Tradition. The Widow Twankey was a woman.

DI Grimble made his arrest and the case against Denis Timson was dropped by the Crown Prosecution Service. As spring came to the Temple gardens, Hilda opened a letter in the other case which had turned on the recognition of old, familiar faces and read it out to me.

"The repointing's going well on the tower and we hope to have it finished by Easter," Poppy Longstaff had written. "And I have to tell you, Hilda, the oil-fired heating has changed our lives. Eric says it's like living in the tropics. Cooking supper last night I had to peel off one of my cardigans." She Who Must Be Obeyed put down the letter from her old school friend and said, thoughtfully, "Noblesse oblige."

"What was that, Hilda?"

"I could tell at once that Donald Compton was a true gentleman. The sort that does good by stealth. Of course, poor old Eric thought he'd never get the tower mended, but I somehow felt that Donald wouldn't fail him. It was noblesse."

"Perhaps it was," I conceded, "but in this case the noblesse was Rumpole's."

"Rumpole! What on earth do you mean? You hardly paid to have the church tower repointed, did you?"

"In one sense, yes."

"I can't believe that. After all the years it took you to have the bathroom decorated. What on earth do you mean about your noblesse?"

"It'd take too long to explain, old darling. Besides, I've got a conference in chambers. Tricky case of receiving stolen surgical appliances. I suppose," I added doubtfully, "it may lead, at some time in the distant future, to an act of charity."

Easter came, the work on the tower was successfully completed and I was walking back to chambers after a gruelling day down at the Bailey when I saw, wafting through the Temple cloisters, the unlikely apparition of the Revd Eric Longstaff. He chirruped a greeting and said he'd come up to consult some legal brains on the proper investment of what remained of the Church Restoration Fund.

"I'm so profoundly grateful," he told me, "that I decided to invite you down to the rectory last Christmas."

"*You* decided?"

"Of course I did."

"I thought your wife Poppy extended the invitation to She . . ."

"Oh, yes. But I thought of the idea. It was the result of a good deal of hard knee-work and guidance from above. I knew you were the right man for the job."

"What job?"

"The Compton job."

What was this? The rector was speaking like an old con. The Coldsands caper? "What *can* you mean?"

"I just mean that I knew you'd defended Donald Compton. In a previous existence."

"How on earth did you know that?"

Eric drew himself up to his full, willowy height. "I'm not a prison visitor for nothing," he said proudly. "I thought you were just the chap to put the fear of God into him. You were the very person to put the squeeze on the Lord of the Manor."

"Put the squeeze on him?" Words were beginning to fail me.

"That was the idea. It came to me as a result of knee-work."

"So you brought us down to that freezing rectory just so I could blackmail the local benefactor?"

"Didn't it turn out well!"

"May the Lord forgive you."

"He's very forgiving."

"Next time," I spoke to the Man of God severely, "the Church can do its blackmailing for itself."

"Oh, we're quite used to that." The rector smiled at me in what I thought was a lofty manner. "Particularly around Christmas."

Rumpole and the Christmas Break

I

"We must be constantly on guard. Night and day. Vigilance is essential. I'm sure you would agree, wouldn't you, Luci?"

Soapy Sam Ballard, our always-nervous Head of Chambers, addressed the meeting as though the forces of evil were already beating on the doors of 4 Equity Court, and weapons of mass destruction had laid waste to the dining hall, condemning us to a long winter of cold meat and sandwiches. As usual, he longed for confirmation and turned to our recently appointed Head of Marketing and Administration, who was now responsible for the chambers' image.

"Quite right, Chair." Luci's North Country voice sounded quietly amused, as though she didn't take the alarming state of the world quite as seriously as Ballard did.

"Thank you for your contribution, Luci." Soapy Sam, it seemed, thought she might have gone a little further, such as recommending that Securicor mount a twenty-four-hour guard on the Head of Chambers. Then he added, in a voice of doom, "I have already asked our clerk to keep an extremely sharp eye on the sugar kept in the coffee cupboard."

"Why did you do that?" I ventured to ask our leader. "Has Claude been shovelling it in by the tablespoonful?"

Claude Erskine-Brown was one of the few barristers I have ever met who combined a passionate affection for Wagner's operas with a remarkably sweet tooth, continuously sucking wine gums in court and loading his coffee with heaped spoonfuls of sugar.

"It's not that, Rumpole." Soapy Sam was getting petulant. "It's anthrax."

"What anthrax?"

"The sugar might be. There are undoubtedly people out there who are out to get us, Rumpole. Haven't you been listening at all to government warnings?"

"I seem to remember them telling us one day that if we

went down the Tube we'd all be gassed, and the next day they said, 'Sorry, we were only joking. Carry on going down the Tube.'"

"Rumpole! Do you take nothing seriously?"

"Some things," I assured Soapy Sam. "But not the Government."

"We are," here Ballard ignored me as an apparently hopeless case, and addressed the meeting, "especially vulnerable."

"Why's that?" I was curious enough to ask.

"We represent the law, Rumpole. The centre of a civilized society. Naturally we'd be high on their hit list."

"You mean the Houses of Parliament, Buckingham Palace and Number 4 Equity Court? I wonder, you may be right."

"I propose to appoint a small chambers emergency committee consisting of myself, Claude Erskine-Brown and Archie Prosser. Please report to one of us if you notice anything unusual or out of the ordinary. I assume you have nothing to report, Rumpole?"

"Nothing much. I did notice a chap on the Tube. A fellow of Middle Eastern appearance wearing a turban and a beard and muttering into a Dictaphone. He got out at South Kensington. I don't suppose it's important."

Just for a moment, I thought—indeed, I hoped—our Head of Chambers looked at me as though he believed what I had said, but then justifiable doubt overcame him.

"Very funny," Ballard told the meeting. "But then you can scarcely afford to be serious about the danger we're all in, can you, Rumpole? Considering you're defending one of these maniacs."

"Rumpole would defend anyone," said Archie Prosser—the newest arrival in our chambers—who had an ill-deserved reputation as a wit.

"If you mean anyone who's put on trial and tells me they're innocent, then the answer is yes."

Nothing alarming happened on the Tube on my way home that evening, except for the fact that, owing to a "work to rule" by the drivers, the train gave up work at Victoria and I had to walk the rest of the way home to Froxbury Mansions in the Gloucester Road. The shops and their windows were full of glitter, artificial snow and wax models perched on sleighs wearing party dresses. Taped carols came tinkling out of Tesco's. The chambers meeting had been the last of the term, and the Old Bailey had interrupted its business for the season of peace and goodwill.

There was very little of either in the case which I had been doing in front of the aptly named Mr Justice Graves. Mind you, I would have had a fairly rough ride before the most reasonable of judges. Even some compassionate old darlings like Mr Justice "Pussy" Proudfoot might have regarded my client with something like horror and been tempted to dismiss my speech to the jury as a hopeless attempt to prevent a certain conviction and a probable sentence of not less than thirty years. The murder we had been considering, when we were interrupted by Christmas, had been cold-blooded and merciless, and there was clear evidence that it had been the work of a religious fanatic.

The victim, Honoria Glossop, Professor of Comparative Religion at William Morris University in East London, had been the author of a number of books, including her latest, and last, publication *Sanctified Killing—A History of Religious Warfare.* She had been severely critical of all acts of violence and aggression—including the Inquisition and the Crusades—committed in the name of God. She had also included a chapter on Islam which spoke scathingly of some ayatollahs and the cruelties committed by Islamic fundamentalists.

It was this chapter which had caused my client, a young student of computer technology at William Morris named Hussein Khan, to issue a private fatwa. He composed, on one of the university computers, a letter to Professor Glossop announcing that her blasphemous references to the religious leaders of his country deserved nothing less than death—which would inevitably catch up with her. Then he left the letter in her pigeonhole.

It took very little time for the authorship of the letter to be discovered. Hussein Khan was sent down from William Morris and began spending his time helping his family in the Star of Persia restaurant they ran in Golders Green. A week later, Professor Glossop, who had been working late in her office at the university, was found slumped across her desk, having been shot at close quarters by a bullet from a revolver of Czech origins, the sort of weapon which is readily and cheaply available in certain South London pubs. Beside her on the desk, now stained with her blood, was the letter containing the sentence of death.

Honoria and her husband Richard "Ricky" Glossop lived in what the estate agents would describe as "a three-million-pound town house in the Boltons." The professor had, it seemed, inherited a great deal of money from a family business in the Midlands which allowed her to pursue her academic career, and Ricky to devote his life to country sports without the need for gainful employment. He was clearly, from his photographs in the papers, an outstandingly handsome figure, perhaps five or six years younger than his wife. After her murder, he received, and everyone felt deserved, huge public sympathy. He and Honoria had met when they were both guests on a yacht touring the Greek Islands, and she had chosen him and his good looks in preference to all the available professors and academic authors she knew. In spite of their differences in age and interests, they seemed to have lived happily together for ten years until, so the prosecution said, death overtook Honoria Glossop in the person of my now universally hated client.

Such was the case I was engaged in at the Old Bailey in the run-up to Christmas. There were no tidings of great joy to report. The cards were stacked dead against me, and at every stage it looked like I was losing, trumped by a judge who regarded defence barristers as flies on the tasty dish of justice.

Mr Justice Graves, known to me only as "The Old Gravestone," had a deep, sepulchral voice and the general appearance of a man waking up with an upset stomach on a wet weekend. He had clearly come to the conclusion that the world was full of irredeemable sinners. The nearest thing to a smile I had seen on the face of The Old Gravestone was the look of grim delight he had displayed when, after a difficult case, the jury had come back with the guilty verdict he had clearly longed for.

So, as you can imagine, the atmosphere in Court Number One at the Old Bailey during the trial of the Queen against Hussein Kahn was about as warm as the South Pole during a blizzard. The Queen may have adopted a fairly detached attitude towards my client, but the judge certainly hadn't.

The prosecution was in the not altogether capable hands of Soapy Sam Ballard, which was why he had practically named me as a founding member of Al Qaeda at our chambers meeting. His junior was the newcomer Archie Prosser.

These two might not have been the most deadly optimists I had ever had to face during my long career at the Bar, but a first-year law student with a lowish IQ would, I thought, have had little difficulty in securing a conviction against the young student who had managed to become one of the most hated men in England.

As he was brought up from the cells and placed in the dock between two prison officers, the jury took one brief, appalled look at him and then turned their eyes on what seemed to them to be the less offensive figure of Soapy Sam as he prepared to open his devastating case.

So I sat at my end of counsel's benches. The brief had been offered to several QCs ("Queer Customers" I always call them), but they had excused themselves as being too busy, or unwell, or going on holiday—any excuse to avoid being cast as leading counsel for the forces of evil. It was only, it seemed, Rumpole who stuck to the old-fashioned belief that the most outrageous sinner deserves to have his defence, if he had one, put fairly and squarely in front of a jury.

Mr Justice Gravestone didn't share my views. When Ballard rose he was greeted with something almost like a smile from the bench, and his most obvious comments were underlined by a judicious nod followed by a careful note underlined in the judicial notebook. Every time I rose to cross-examine a prosecution witness, however, Graves sighed heavily and laid down his pencil as though nothing of any significance was likely to emerge.

This happened when I had a few pertinent questions to ask the pathologist, my old friend Professor Arthur Ackerman, forensic scientist and master of the morgues. After he had given his evidence about the cause of death (pretty obvious), I started off.

"You say, Professor Ackerman, that the shot was fired at close quarters?"

"Yes, Mr Rumpole. Indeed it was." Ackerman and I had been through so many bloodstained cases together that we chatted across the court like old friends.

"You told us," I went on, "that the bullet entered the deceased's neck—she was probably shot from behind—and that, among other things, the bullet severed an artery."

"That is so."

"So, as a result, blood spurted over the desk. We know it was on the letter. Would you have expected the person, whoever it was, who shot her at close quarters to have had some blood on his clothing?"

"I think that may well have happened."

"Would you say it probably happened?"

"Probably. Yes."

When I got this answer from the witness, I stood awhile in silence, looking at the motionless judge.

"Is that all you have to ask, Mr Rumpole?"

"No, My Lord. I'm waiting so Your Lordship has time to make note of the evidence. I see Your Lordship's pencil is taking a rest!"

"I'm sure the jury has heard your questions, Mr Rumpole. And the answers."

"I'm sure they have, and you will no doubt remind them of that during your summing up. So I'm sure Your Lordship will wish to make a note."

Gravestone, with an ill grace, picked up his pencil and made the shortest possible note. Then I asked Ackerman my last question.

"And I take it you know that the clothes my client wore that evening were minutely examined and no traces of any bloodstains were found?"

"My Lord, how can this witness know what was on Khan's clothing?" Soapy Sam objected.

"Quite right, Mr Ballard," the judge was quick to agree. "That was an outrageous question, Mr Rumpole. The jury will disregard it."

It got no better. I rose, at the end of a long day in court, to cross-examine Superintendent Gregory, the perfectly decent officer in charge of the case.

"My client, Mr Khan, made no secret of the fact that he had written this threatening letter, did he, Superintendent Gregory?"

"He did not, My Lord," Gregory answered with obvious satisfaction.

"In fact," said Mr Justice Graves, searching among his notes, "the witness Sadiq told us that your client boasted to him of the fact in the university canteen."

There, at last, The Gravestone had overstepped the mark.

"He didn't say 'boasted.'"

Soapy Sam Ballard QC, the alleged Head of our Chambers, got up with his notebook at the ready.

"Sadiq said that Khan told him he had written the letter and, in answer to Your Lordship, that 'he seemed to feel no sort of guilt about it.'"

"There you are, Mr Rumpole." Graves also seemed to feel no sort of guilt. "Doesn't that come to exactly the same thing?"

"Certainly not, My Lord. The word 'boasted' was never used."

"The jury may come to the conclusion that it amounted to boasting."

"They may indeed, My Lord. But that's for them to decide, without directions from Your Lordship."

"Mr Rumpole," here the judge adopted an expression of

lofty pity, "I realize you have many difficulties in this case. But perhaps we may proceed without further argument. Have you any more questions for this officer?"

"Just one, My Lord." I turned to the superintendent. "This letter was traced to one of the university word processors."

"That is so, yes."

"You would agree that my client took no steps at all to cover up the fact that he was the author of this outrageous threat."

"He seems to have been quite open about it, yes."

"That's hardly consistent with the behaviour of someone about to commit a brutal murder, is it?"

"I suppose it was a little surprising, yes," Jack Gregory was fair enough to admit.

"Very surprising, isn't it? And of course by the time this murder took place, everyone knew he had written the letter. He'd been sent down for doing so."

"That's right."

The Gravestone intervened. "Did it not occur to you, Superintendent Gregory, that being sent down might have provided an additional motive for the murder?"

The judge clearly thought he was on to something, and was deeply gratified when the superintendent answered, "That might have been so, My Lord."

"That might have been so," Graves dictated to himself as

he wrote the answer down. Then he thought of another point that might be of use to the hardly struggling prosecution. "Of course, if a man thinks he's justified, for religious or moral reasons, in killing someone, he might have no inhibitions about boasting of the fact?"

I knew it. Soapy Sam must have known it, and the jury had better be told it. The judge had gone too far. I rose to my feet, as quickly as my weight and the passage of the years would allow, and uttered a sharp protest.

"My Lord, the prosecution is in the able hands of Samuel Ballard QC. I'm sure he can manage to present the case against my client without Your Lordship's continued help and encouragement."

This was followed by a terrible silence, the sort of stillness that precedes a storm.

"Mr Rumpole." His Lordship's words were as warm as hailstones. "That was a most outrageous remark."

"It was a point I felt I should make," I told him, "in fairness to my client."

"As I have said, I realize you have an extremely difficult case to argue, Mr Rumpole." Once more Graves was reminding the jury that I was on a certain loser. "But I cannot overlook your inappropriate and disrespectful attitude towards the court. I shall have to consider whether your conduct should be reported to the proper authority."

After these dire remarks and a few more unimportant questions to the superintendent, Graves turned to the jury and reminded them that this no doubt painful and shocking case would be resumed after the Christmas break. He said this in the solemn and sympathetic tones of someone announcing the death of a dear friend or relative, then he wished them a "Happy Christmas."

The Tube train for home was packed and I stood, swaying uneasily, sandwiched between an eighteen-stone man in a donkey jacket with a heavy cold and an elderly woman with a pair of the sharpest elbows I have ever encountered on the Circle Line.

No doubt all of the other passengers had hard, perhaps unrewarding, lives but they didn't have to spend their days acting as a sort of human buffer between a possibly fatal fanatic and a hostile judge who certainly wanted to end the career of the inconveniently argumentative Rumpole. The train, apparently as exhausted as I felt, ground to a halt between Embankment and Westminster, and as the lights went out I'd almost decided to give up the Bar. Then the lights glowed again faintly and the train jerked on. I supposed I would have to go on as well—wouldn't I?—not being the sort of character who could retire to the country and plant strawberries.

When I reached the so-called "Mansion Flat" in the Gloucester Road I was, I have to say, not a little surprised by the warmth of the welcome I received. My formidable wife Hilda, known to me only as "She Who Must Be Obeyed" said, "Sit down, Rumpole. You look tired out." And she lit the gas fire. A few minutes later, she brought me a glass of my usual refreshment—the very ordinary claret available from Pommeroy's Wine Bar in Fleet Street, a vintage known to me as "Château Thames Embankment." I suspected that all this attention meant that she had some uncomfortable news to break and I was right.

"This year," she told me, with the firmness of The Old Gravestone pronouncing judgement, "I'm not going to do Christmas. It's getting too much for me."

Christmas was not usually much of a "do" in the Rumpole household. There is the usual exchange of presents; I get a tie and Hilda receives the statutory bottle of lavender water, which seems to be for laying down rather than immediate use. She cooks the turkey and I open the Château Thames Embankment, and so our Saviour's birth is celebrated.

"I have booked us this year," Hilda announced, "into Cherry Picker's Hall. You look in need of a rest, Rumpole."

What was this place she spoke of? A retirement home? Sheltered accommodation? "I'm in the middle of an important murder. I can't pack up and go into a home."

"It's not a home, Rumpole. It's a country house hotel. In the Cotswolds. They're doing a special offer—four nights with full board. A children's party. Christmas lunch with crackers and a dance on Christmas Eve. It'll be something to look forward to."

"I don't really think so. We haven't got any children and I don't want to dance at Christmas. So shall we say no to the Cherry Picker's?"

"Whether you dance or not is entirely up to you, Rumpole. But you can't say no because I've already booked it and paid the deposit. And I've collected your old dinner jacket from the cleaners."

So I was unusually silent. Not for nothing is my wife entitled "She Who Must Be Obeyed."

I was unusually silent on the way to the Cotswolds too, but as we approached this country house hotel, I felt that perhaps, after all, She Who Must Be Obeyed had made a wise decision and that the considerable financial outlay on the "Budget Christmas Offer" might turn out, in spite of all my apprehensions, to be justified.

We took a taxi from the station. As we made our way down deep into the countryside, the sun was shining and the trees were throwing a dark pattern against a clear sky. We passed green fields where cows were munching and a stream trickling over rocks. A stray deer crossed the road in front of us and a single kite (at least, Hilda said it was a kite) wheeled across the sky. We had, it seemed, entered a better, more peaceful world far from the problems of terrorists, the bloodstained letter containing a sentence of death, the impossible client and the no less difficult judge I struggled with down at the Old Bailey. In spite of all my troubles, I felt a kind of contentment stealing over me.

Happily, the contentment only deepened as our taxi scrunched the gravel by the entrance to Cherry Picker's Hall. The old grey stones of the one-time manor house were gilded by the last of the winter sun. We were greeted warmly by a friendly manageress and our things were taken up to a comfortable room overlooking a wintry garden. Then, in no time at all, I was sitting by a blazing log fire in the residents' lounge, eating anchovy paste sandwiches with the prospect of a dark and alcoholic fruit cake to follow. Even my appalling client, Hussein Khan, might, I thought, if brought into such an environment, forget his calling as a messenger of terror and relax after dinner.

"It's wonderful to be away from the Old Bailey. I just had the most terrible quarrel with a particularly unlearned judge," I told Hilda, who was reading a back number of *Country Life*.

"You keep quarrelling with judges, don't you? Why don't you take up fishing, Rumpole? Lazy days by a trout stream might help you forget all those squalid cases you do." She had clearly got to the country sports section of the magazine.

"This quarrel went a bit further than usual. He threatened to report me for professional misconduct. I didn't like the way he kept telling the jury my client was guilty."

"Well, isn't he guilty, Rumpole?" In all innocence, Hilda had asked the awkward question.

"Well. Quite possibly. But that's for the jury of twelve honest citizens to decide, not Mr Justice Gravestone."

"Gravestone? Is that his name?"

"No. His name's Graves. I call him Gravestone."

"You would, wouldn't you, Rumpole?"

"He speaks like a voice from the tomb. It's my personal belief that he urinates iced water!"

"Really, Rumpole. Do try not to be vulgar. So what did you say to Mr Justice Graves? You might as well tell me the truth."

She was right, of course. The only way of appeasing She Who Must was to plead guilty and throw oneself on the mercy of the court. "I told him to come down off the bench and join Soapy Sam Ballard on the prosecution team."

"Rumpole, that was terribly rude of you!"

"Yes," I said, with considerable satisfaction. "It really was."

"So no wonder he's cross with you."

"Very cross indeed." Once again I couldn't keep the note of triumph out of my voice.

"I should think he probably hates you, Rumpole."

"I should think he probably does."

"Well, you're safe here anyway. You can forget all about your precious Mr Justice Gravestone and just enjoy Christmas."

She was, as usual, right. I stretched my legs towards the fire and took a gulp of Earl Grey and a large bite of rich, dark cake.

And then I heard a voice call out, a voice from the tomb.

"Rumpole!" it said. "What an extraordinary coincidence. Are you here for Christmas? You and your good lady?"

I turned my head. I had not, alas, been mistaken. There he was, in person—Mr Justice Gravestone. He was wearing a tweed suit and some type of regimental or old school tie. His usually lugubrious features wore the sort of smile only previously stimulated by a long succession of guilty verdicts. And the next thing he said came as such a surprise that I almost choked on my slice of fruit cake.

"I say," he said, and I promise you these were Gravestone's exact words, "this is fun, isn't it?"

I I

"I've often wondered what it would be like to be married to Rumpole."

It was a lie, of course. I dare swear that the Honourable Gravestone never spent one minute of his time wondering what it would be like to be Mrs Rumpole. But there he was, having pulled up a chair, tucking into our anchovy paste sandwiches and smiling at She Who Must Be Obeyed with as much joy as if she had just returned twenty guilty verdicts—one of them being in the case of the Judge versus Rumpole.

"He can be a bit difficult at times, of course," Hilda weighed in for the prosecution.

"A little difficult! That's putting it mildly, Mrs Rumpole. You can't imagine the trouble we have with him in court."

To my considerable irritation, my wife and the judge were smiling together as though they were discussing, with tolerant amusement, the irrational behaviour of a difficult child.

"Of course we mustn't discuss the case before me at the moment," Graves said.

"That ghastly terrorist." Hilda had already reached a verdict.

"Exactly! We won't say a word about him."

"Just as well," Hilda agreed. "We get far too much discussion of Rumpole's cases."

"Really? Poor Mrs Rumpole." The judge gave her a look of what I found to be quite sickening sympathy. "Brings his work home with him, does he?"

"Oh, absolutely! He'll do anything in the world for some ghastly murderer or other, but can I get him to help me redecorate the bathroom?"

"You redecorate bathrooms?" The judge looked at Hilda with admiration as though she had just admitted to sailing round the world in a hot air balloon. Then he turned to me. "You're a lucky man, Rumpole!"

"He won't tell you that." Hilda was clearly enjoying our Christmas break even more than she had expected. "By the way, I hope he wasn't too rude to you in court."

"I thought we weren't meant to discuss the case," I tried to make an objection, which was entirely disregarded by my wife and the unlearned judge.

"Oh, that wasn't Rumpole being merely rude. It was Rumpole trying to impress his client by showing him how fearlessly he can stand up to judges. We're quite used to that."

"He says," Hilda still seemed to find the situation amusing, "that you threatened to report him for professional misconduct. You really ought to be more careful, shouldn't you, Rumpole?"

"Oh, I said that," Graves had the audacity to admit, "just to give your husband a bit of a shock. He did go a little green, I thought, when I made the suggestion."

"I did not go green!" By now I was losing patience with the judge Hilda was treating like a long-lost friend. "I made a perfectly reasonable protest against a flagrant act of premature adjudication! You had obviously decided that my client is guilty and you were going to let the jury know it."

"But isn't he guilty, Rumpole? Isn't that obvious?"

"Of course he's not guilty. He's completely innocent. And will remain so until the jury come back into court and convict him. And that is to be their decision. And what the judge wants will have absolutely nothing to do with it!"

I may have gone too far, but I felt strongly on the subject. Judge Graves, however, seemed completely impervious to my attack. He stood, still smiling, warming his tweed-covered backside at the fire and repeated, "We really mustn't discuss the case we're involved in at the moment. Let's remember, it is Christmas."

"Yes, Rumpole. It is Christmas." Hilda had cast herself, it seemed, as Little Lady Echo to His Lordship.

"That's settled, then. Look, why don't I book a table for three at dinner?" The judge was still smiling. "Wouldn't that be tremendous fun?"

. . .

"What a perfectly charming man Judge Graves is."

These were words I never expected to hear spoken, but they contained the considered verdict of She Who Must Be Obeyed before we settled down for the first night of our Christmas holiday. The food at dinner had been simple but good. (The entrecôte steak had not been arranged in a little tower swamped by tomato coulis and there had been a complete absence of rocket and all the idiocy of smart restaurants.) The Gravestone was clearly on the most friendly of terms with "Lorraine," the manageress, and he and Hilda enjoyed a lengthy conversation on the subject of fishing, which sport Graves practised and on which Hilda was expert after her study of the back number of *Country Life* in the residents' lounge.

Now and again I was asked why I didn't go out on a day's fishing with Hilda's newfound friend the judge, a question I found as easy to answer as "Why don't you take part in the London Marathon wearing nothing but bikini bottoms and a wig?" For a greater part of the dinner I had sat, unusually silent, listening to the ceaseless chatter of the newfound friends, feeling as superfluous as a maiden aunt at a lovers' meeting.

Soon after telling me how charming she had found The Gravestone, Hilda sank into a deep and contented sleep. As the moonlight streamed in at the window and I heard the faraway hooting of an owl, I began to worry about the case we hadn't discussed at dinner.

I couldn't forget my first meeting in Brixton Prison with my client, Hussein Khan. Although undoubtedly the author of the fatal letter, he didn't seem, when I met him in the company of my faithful solicitor Bonny Bernard, to be the sort who would strike terror into the heart of anyone. He was short and unsmiling with soft brown eyes, a quiet monotonous voice and unusually small hands. He wasn't only uncomplaining, he seemed to find it the most natural thing in the world that he should find himself locked up and facing the most serious of all charges. It was, he told us early in the interview, the will of Allah, and if Allah willed, who was he, a twenty-two-year-old undergraduate in computer studies, to ask questions? I was, throughout the case, amazed at the combination, in my inexplicable client, of the most complicated knowledge of modern technology and the most primitive and merciless religious beliefs.

"I wrote the letter. Of course I did. It was not my decision that she should die. It was the will of God."

"The will of God that a harmless woman should be shot for writing something critical in a book?"

"Die for blasphemy, yes."

"And they say you were her executioner, that you carried out the sentence."

"I didn't do that." He was looking at me patiently, as though I still had much to learn about the faith of Hussein Khan. "I knew that death would come to her in time. It came sooner than I had expected."

So, was I defending a man who had issued a death threat which had then been obediently carried out by some person or persons unknown in the peaceful precincts of an East London university? It seemed an unlikely story, and I had not been looking forward to the murder trial which started at the Old Bailey during the run-up to Christmas.

At the heart of the case there was, I thought, a mystery. The letter, I knew, was clear evidence of Hussein's guilt, and yet there was no forensic evidence—no bloodstains on his clothing, no traces of his having fired a pistol with a silencer (there must have been a silencer, because no one in the building had heard a shot). This was evidence in Hussein's favour, but I had to remember that he had been in the university building when the murder had taken place, although he'd already been sent down for writing the letter.

As the owl hooted, Hilda breathed deeply. Sleep eluded me. I went through Hussein Khan's story again. He had received a phone call, he said, when he was at his parents' restaurant. (He had answered the phone himself, so there was no one to confirm the call.) It had been, it seemed, from a girl who said she was the senior tutor's secretary and that the tutor wanted to meet him in the university library at ten o'clock that evening to discuss his future.

He had arrived at the William Morris building at nine thirty and had told Mr Luttrell, the man at the main reception area, that he was there to meet the senior tutor at the library. He said that when he had arrived at the library, the tutor wasn't there and that he had waited for over an hour and then gone home, having never been near Honoria Glossop's office.

Of course the senior tutor and his secretary denied that either had made such a telephone call. The implication was that Hussein was lying through his teeth and that he had gone to the university because he had known that Professor Glossop worked in her office until late at night and he had intended to kill her.

At last I fell into a restless sleep. In my dreams I saw myself being prosecuted by Soapy Sam Ballard who was wearing a long beard and arguing for my conviction under sharia law.

I woke early to the first faint flush of daylight as a distant cock crowed. I got up, tiptoed across the room and extracted from the bottom of my case the papers in *R. v. Khan*. I was looking for the answer to a problem as yet undefined, going through the prosecution statement again and finding nothing very much.

I reminded myself that Mr Luttrell, at his reception desk, had seen Honoria and her husband arrive together and go to her office. Ricky Glossop had left not more than fifteen minutes later, and later still he had telephoned and couldn't get an answer from his wife. He had asked Luttrell to go to Honoria's office because she wasn't answering her phone. The receptionist had gone to her office and found her lying across her desk, her hand close to the bloodstained letter.

Next I read the statement from Honoria's secretary, Sue Blackmore, describing how she had found the letter in Honoria's university pigeonhole and taken it to Honoria at her home. Of Honoria's reaction on receiving it, Ms Blackmore commented, "She didn't take the note all that seriously and wouldn't even tell the police." Ricky Glossop had finally rung the anti-terrorist department in Scotland Yard and showed them the letter.

None of this was new. There was only one piece of evidence which I might have overlooked.

In the senior tutor's statement he said he had spoken to Honoria on the morning of the day she had died. She had told him that she couldn't be at a seminar that afternoon because she had "an urgent appointment with Tony Hawkin." Hawkin, as the senior tutor knew, was a solicitor who acted for the university, and had also acted for Honoria Glossop in a private capacity. The senior tutor had no idea why she had wanted to see her solicitor. He never saw his colleague alive again.

I was giving that last document some thought when Hilda stirred, opened an eye and instructed me to ring for breakfast.

"You'll have to look after yourself today, Rumpole," she told me. "Gerald's going to take me fishing for grayling."

"Gerald?" Was there some new man in Hilda's life who had turned up in the Cotswolds?

"You know. The charming judge you introduced me to last night."

"You can't mean Gravestone?"

"Don't be ridiculous. Of course I mean Gerald Graves."

"You're going fishing with him?"

"He's very kindly going to take me to a bit of river he shares with a friend."

"How delightful." I adopted the ironic tone. "If you catch anything, bring it back for supper."

"Oh, I'm not going to do any fishing. I'm simply going to watch Gerald from the bank. He's going to show me how he ties his flies."

"How absolutely fascinating."

She didn't seem to think she'd said anything at all amusing and began to lever herself briskly out of bed.

"Do ring up about that breakfast, Rumpole!" she said. "I've got to get ready for Gerald."

He may be Gerald to you, I thought, but he will always be The Old Gravestone to me.

After Hilda had gone to meet her newfound friend, I finished the bacon and eggs with sausage and fried slice—which I had ordered as an organic, low calorie breakfast—and put a telephone call through to my faithful solicitor Bonny Bernard. I found him at his home talking over a background of shrill and excited children eager for the next morning and the well-filled stockings.

"Mr Rumpole!" The man sounded shocked by my call. "Don't you ever take a day off? It's Christmas Eve!"

"I know it's Christmas Eve. I know that perfectly well," I told him. "And my wife has gone fishing with our sepulchral judge, whom she calls "Gerald." Meanwhile, have you got any close friends or associates working at Hawkin's, the solicitor?"

"Barry Tuck used to be our legal executive—moved there about three years ago."

"A cooperative sort of character is he, Tuck?"

"We got on very well. Yes."

"Then get him to find out why Honoria Glossop went to see Tony Hawkin the afternoon before she was shot. It must have been something fairly urgent. She missed a seminar in order to go."

"Is it important?"

"Probably not, but it just might be something we ought to know."

"I hope you're enjoying your Christmas break, Mr Rumpole."

"Quite enjoying it. I'd like it better without a certain member of the judiciary. Oh, and I've got a hard time ahead."

"Working?"

"No," I told my patient solicitor gloomily. "Dancing."

"Quick, quick, slow, Rumpole. That's better. Now chassé! Don't you remember, Rumpole? This is where you chassé."

The truth was that I remembered little about it. It had been so long ago. How many years could it have been since Hilda and I had trodden across a dance floor? Yet here I was in a dinner jacket, which was now uncomfortably tight around the waist, doing my best to walk round this small area of polished parquet in time to the music with one arm around Hilda's satin-covered waist and my other hand gripping one of hers. Although for much of the time she was walking backwards, she was undoubtedly the one in command of the enterprise. I heard a voice singing, seemingly from far off, above the music of the five-piece band laid on for the hotel's dinner dance. It was a strange sound and one that I hadn't heard for what seemed many years—She Who Must Be Obeyed was singing. I looked towards my table, rather as someone lost at sea might look towards a distant shore, and I saw Mr Justice Gravestone smiling at us with approval.

"Well done, Hilda! And you came through that quite creditably, I thought, Rumpole. I mean, at least you managed to remain upright, although there were a few dodgy moments coming round that far corner."

"That was when I told him chassé. Rumpole couldn't quite manage it."

As they were both enjoying a laugh I realized that, during a long day by the river which had, it seemed, produced nothing more than two fish so small that they had had to be returned to their natural environment, Mrs Rumpole had become "Hilda" to the judge, who had already become "Gerald."

"You know, when you retire, Rumpole," the judge was sounding sympathetic in the most irritating kind of way, "you could take dancing lessons."

"There's so much Rumpole could do *if* he retired. I keep telling him," was Hilda's contribution. "He could have wonderful days like we had, Gerald. Outdoors, close to nature and fishing."

"Catching two small grayling you had to put back in the

water?" I was bold enough to ask. "It would've been easier to pay a quick visit to the fishmonger's."

"Catching fish is not the point of fishing," Hilda told me.

Before I could ask her what the point of it was, the judge came up with a suggestion. "When you retire, I could teach you fishing, Rumpole. We could have a few days out together."

"Now, then. Isn't that kind of Gerald, Rumpole?" Hilda beamed and I had to mutter, "Very kind," although the judge's offer had made me more determined than ever to die with my wig on.

It was at this point that Lorraine the manageress came to the judge with a message. He read it quickly and then said, "Poor old Leslie Mulliner. You know him, don't you, Rumpole? He sits in the Chancery Division."

I had to confess I didn't know anyone who sat in the Chancery Division.

"He was going to join us here tomorrow but his wife's not well."

"He said on the phone that you'd do the job for him tomorrow." Lorraine seemed anxious.

"Yes, of course," Graves hurried to reassure her. "I'll stand in for him."

Before I could get any further explanation of the "job," the music had struck up a more contemporary note. Foxtrots were out, and with a cry of "Come along, Hilda" Graves was strutting the dance floor, making curious rhythmic movements with his hands. And Hilda, walking free and unfastened from her partner, was also strutting and waving her arms, smiling with pleasure. It wasn't, I'm sure, the most up-to-date form of dancing, but it was, I suppose, a gesture from two sedate citizens who were doing their best to become, for a wine-filled moment on Christmas Eve, a couple of teenagers.

Christmas Day at Cherry Picker's Hall was uneventful. The judge suggested church, and I stood while he and Hilda bellowed out "O come, all ye faithful . . ." Then we sat among the faithful under the Norman arches, beside the plaques and monuments to so many vanished rectors and country squires, looking out upon the holly around the pulpit and the flowers on the altar. I tried to understand, not for the first time, how a religious belief could become so perverted as to lead to death threats, terror and a harmless professor shot through the head.

We had lunch in a pub and then the judge announced he had work to do and left us.

After a long and satisfactory sleep, Hilda and I woke around teatime and went to the residents' lounge. Long before we got to the door, we could hear the excited cries of children, and when we went in we saw them crowded round the Christmas tree. And there, stooping among the presents, was the expected figure in a red dressing gown (trimmed with white fur), wellington boots, a white beard and a long red hat. As he picked up a present and turned towards us, I felt that fate had played the greatest practical joke it could have thought up to enliven the festive season.

Standing in for his friend Mulliner from the Chancery Division, the sepulchral, unforgiving, prosecution-minded Mr Justice Gravestone, my old enemy, had become Father Christmas.

On Boxing Day, I rang a persistent, dogged, ever useful private detective who, sickened by divorce, now specialized in the cleaner world of crime—Ferdinand Ian Gilmour Newton, known in legal circles as "Fig Newton." I told him that, as was the truth, my wife Hilda was planning a long country walk and lunch in a distant village with a judge whom I had spent a lifetime trying to avoid. And I asked him, if he had no previous engagements, if he'd like to sample the table d'hôte at Cherry Picker's Hall.

Fig Newton is a lugubrious character of indeterminate age, usually dressed in an old mackintosh and an even older hat, with a drip at the end of his nose caused by a seemingly perpetual cold—most likely caught while keeping observation in all weathers. But today he had shed his outer garments, his nose was dry and he was tucking into the lamb cutlets with something approaching enthusiasm. "Bit of a step up from your usual pub lunch, this, isn't it, Mr Rumpole?"

"It certainly is, Fig. We're splashing out this Christmas. Now this case I'm doing down the Bailey . . ."

"The terrorist?"

"Yes, the terrorist."

"You're on to a loser with that one, Mr Rumpole." Fig was gloomily relishing the fact.

"Most probably. All the same, there are a few stones I don't want to leave unturned."

"Such as what?"

"Find out what you can about the Glossops."

"The dead woman's family?"

"That's right. See what's known about their lives, hobbies, interests. That sort of thing. I need to get more of a picture of their lives together. Oh, and see if the senior tutor knows more about the Glossops. Pick up any gossip going around the university. I'll let you know if Bonny Bernard has found out why Honoria had a date with her solicitor."

"So when do you want all this done by, Mr Rumpole?" Fig picked up a cutlet bone and chewed gloomily. "Tomorrow morning, I suppose?"

"Oh, sooner than that if possible," I told him.

It was not that I felt that the appalling Hussein Khan

had a defence—in fact he might well turn out to have no defence at all. But something at the children's Christmas party had suggested a possibility to my mind.

That something was the sight of Mr Justice Graves standing in for someone else.

III

Christmas was over, and I wondered if the season of goodwill was over with it. The Christmas cards had left the mantelpiece, the holly and the mistletoe had been tidied away, we had exchanged green fields for Gloucester Road and Cherry Picker's Hall was nothing but a memory. The judge was back on the bench to steer the case of *R. v. Khan* towards its inevitable guilty verdict.

The Christmas decorations were not all that had gone. Gerald the cheerful dinner guest, Gerald the energetic dancing partner of She Who Must Be Obeyed, Gerald the fisherman and, in particular, Gerald as Santa Claus had all gone as well, leaving behind only the old thin-lipped, unsmiling Mr Justice Gravestone with the voice of doom, determined to make a difficult case harder than ever.

All the same there was something of a spring in the Rumpole step. This was not only the result of the Christmas break but also due to a suspicion that the case *R. v. Khan* might not be quite as horrifyingly simple as it had at first appeared.

As I crossed the hall on my way to Court Number One, I saw Ricky Glossop—the dashingly handsome husband of the murdered professor—with a pretty blonde girl whom I took to be Sue Blackmore, Honoria's secretary, who was due to give evidence about her employer's reception of the fatal letter. She seemed, so far as I could tell from a passing examination, to be a girl on the verge of a nervous breakdown. She lit a cigarette with trembling fingers, then almost immediately stamped it out. She kept looking, with a kind of desperation, towards the door of the court, and then turning, with a sob, to Ricky Glossop and choking out what I took to be some sort of complaint. He had laid a consoling hand on hers and was talking in the sort of low, exaggeratedly calm tone that a dentist uses when he says, "This isn't going to hurt."

The medical and police evidence had been disposed of before Christmas and now, in the rather strange order adopted by Soapy Sam Ballard for the prosecution, the only witnesses left were Arthur Luttrell (who manned the reception desk), Ricky Glossop and the nervous secretary.

Luttrell, the receptionist, was a smart, precise, self-important man with a sharp nose and a sandy moustache who clearly regarded his position as being at the centre of the university organization. He remembered Hussein Khan coming at nine thirty that evening, saying he had an appointment with the senior tutor and going up to the library. At quarter to ten the Glossops had arrived. Ricky had gone with his wife to her office, but had left about fifteen minutes later. "He stopped to speak to me on the way out," Luttrell told Soapy Sam, "which is why I remember it well."

After that, the evening at William Morris University followed its horrible course. Around eleven o'clock, Hussein Khan left, complaining that he had wasted well over an hour, no senior tutor had come to talk to him and that he was going back to his parents' restaurant in Golders Green. After that Ricky telephoned the reception desk saying that he couldn't get any reply from his wife's office and would Mr Luttrell please go and make sure she was all right. As we all know, Mr Luttrell went to the office, knocked, opened the door and was met by the ghastly spectacle which was to bring us all together in Court Number One at the Old Bailey.

"Mr Rumpole." The judge's tone in calling my name was as aloofly disapproving as though Christmas had never happened. "All this evidence is agreed, isn't it? I don't suppose you'll find it necessary to trouble Mr Luttrell with any questions."

"Just one or two, My Lord."

"Oh, very well." The judge sounded displeased. "Just remember, we're under a public duty not to waste time."

"I hope Your Lordship isn't suggesting that an attempt to get to the truth is a waste of time." And before The Old Gravestone could launch a counter-attack, I asked Mr Luttrell the first question.

"You say Mr Glossop spoke to you on the way out. Can you remember what he said?"

"I remember perfectly." The receptionist looked personally insulted as though I doubted his word. "He asked me if Hussein Khan was in the building."

"He asked you that?"

"Yes, he did."

"And what did you tell him?"

"I told him yes. I said Khan was in the library where he had an appointment with the senior tutor."

I allowed a pause for this curious piece of evidence to sink into the minds of the jury. Graves, of course, filled in the gap by asking if that was my only question.

"Just one more, My Lord."

Here the judge sighed heavily, but I ignored that.

"Are you telling this jury, Mr Luttrell, that Glossop discovered that the man who had threatened his wife with death was in the building, then left without speaking to her again?"

I looked at the jury as I asked this and saw, for the first time in the trial, a few faces looking puzzled.

Mr Luttrell, however, sounded unfazed.

"I've told you what he said. I can't tell you anything more."

"He can't tell us anything more," the judge repeated. "So that would seem to be the end of the matter, wouldn't it, Mr Rumpole?"

"Not quite the end," I told him. "I don't think it's quite the end of the matter yet."

This remark did nothing to improve my relations with His Lordship, who gave me a look from which all traces of the Christmas spirit had been drained.

The jury may have had a moment of doubt during the receptionist's evidence, but when Ricky Glossop was put in the witness box, their sympathy and concern for the good-looking, appealingly modest and stricken husband was obvious. Graves supported them with enthusiasm.

"This is clearly going to be a terrible ordeal for you, Mr Glossop," the judge said, looking at the witness with serious concern. "Wouldn't you like to sit down?"

"No thank you, My Lord. I prefer to stand," Ricky said bravely. The judge gave him the sort of look a commanding officer might give to a young subaltern who'd volunteered to attack the enemy position single-handed. "Just let me know,"

Graves insisted, "if you feel exhausted or overcome by any part of your evidence, and you shall sit down immediately."

"Thank you very much, My Lord. That *is* very kind of Your Lordship."

So, with the formalities of mutual admiration over, Ricky Glossop began to tell his story.

He had met Honoria some ten years before when they were both cruising round the Greek Islands. "She knew all the classical legends and the history of every place. I thought she'd never be bothered with an undereducated slob like me." Here he smiled modestly, and the judge smiled back as a sign of disagreement. "But luckily she put up with me. And, of course, I fell in love with her."

"Of course?" Soapy Sam seemed to feel that this sentence called for some further explanation.

"She was extremely beautiful."

"And she found you attractive?"

"She seemed to. God knows why." This answer earned him smiles for his modesty.

"So you were married for ten years," Ballard said. "And you had no children."

"No. Honoria couldn't have children. It was a great sadness to both of us."

"And how would you describe your marriage up to the time your wife got this terrible letter?" Ballard was holding the letter out, at a distance, as though the paper itself might carry a fatal infection.

"We were very happy."

"When she got the letter, how did she react to it?"

"She was very brave, My Lord," Ricky told the judge. "She said it had obviously been written by some nutcase and that she intended to ignore it."

"She was extremely brave." The judge spoke the words with admiration as he wrote them down.

So Ricky Glossop told his story. And when I—the representative, so it appeared, of his wife's murderer—rose to cross-examine, I felt a chill wind blowing through Court Number One.

"Mr Glossop, you said your marriage to your wife Honoria was a happy one?"

"As far as I was concerned it was very happy." Here he smiled at the jury and some of them nodded back approvingly.

"Did you know that on the afternoon before she was murdered, your wife had consulted a solicitor, Mr Anthony Hawkin of Henshaw and Hawkin?"

"I didn't know that, no."

"Can you guess why?"

"I'm afraid not. My wife had considerable financial interests under her father's will. It might have been about that."

"You mean it might have been about money?"

"Yes."

"Did you know that Anthony Hawkin is well known as an expert on divorce and family law?"

"I didn't know that either."

"And you didn't know that your wife was considering proceedings for divorce?"

"I certainly didn't."

I looked at the jury. They were now, I thought, at least interested. I remembered the frightened blonde girl I had seen outside the court and the hand he had put on hers as he had tried to comfort her.

"Was there any trouble between your wife and yourself because of her secretary, Sue Blackmore?"

"So far as I know, none whatever."

"Mr Rumpole. I'm wondering, and I expect the jury may be wondering as well, what on earth these questions have to do with your client's trial for murder," the judge interjected.

"Then wonder on," I might have quoted Shakespeare to Graves, "till truth make all things plain." But I did not do that. I merely said, "I'm putting these questions to test the credibility of this witness, My Lord."

"And why, Mr Rumpole, are you attacking his credibility? Which part of this gentleman's evidence are you disputing?"

"If I may be allowed to cross-examine in the usual way, I

hope it may become clear," I said, and then I'm afraid I also said, "even to Your Lordship."

At this, Gravestone gave me the look that meant, "You just wait until we come to the summing up, and I'll tell the jury what I think of your attack on this charming husband." But for the moment he remained as silent as a block of ice, so I soldiered on.

"Mr Glossop. Your wife's secretary delivered this threatening letter to her."

"Yes. Honoria was working at home and Sue brought it over from her pigeonhole at the university."

"You've told us that she was very brave, of course. That she had said it was probably from some nutcase and that she intended to ignore it. But you insisted on taking the letter to the police."

"An extremely wise decision, if I may say so," Graves took it upon himself to note.

"And I think you gave the story to the Press Association so that this death threat received wide publicity."

"I thought Honoria would be safer if it was all out in the open. People would be on their guard."

"Another wise decision, the members of the jury might think." Graves was making sure the jury thought it.

"And when the letter was traced to my client, everyone knew that it was Hussein Khan who was the author of the letter?"

"He was dismissed from the university, so I suppose a lot of people knew, yes."

"So, if anything were to have happened to your wife after that, if she were to have been attacked or killed, Hussein Khan would have been the most likely suspect?"

"I think that has been obvious throughout this trial." Graves couldn't resist it.

"My Lord, I'd really much rather get the answers to my questions from the witness than receive them from Your Lordship." I went on quickly before the judge could get in his two pennies' worth. "You took your wife to the university on that fatal night?"

"I often did. If I was going somewhere and she had work to do in her office, I'd drop her off and then collect her later on my way home."

"But you didn't just drop her off, did you? You went inside the building with her. You took her up to her office?"

"Yes. We'd been talking about something in the car and we went on discussing it as I went up to her office with her."

"He escorted her, Mr Rumpole," the sepulchral voice boomed from the bench. "A very gentlemanly thing to do."

"Thank you, My Lord." Ricky's smile was still full of charm.

"And what were you discussing?" I asked him. "Was it divorce?"

"It certainly wasn't divorce. I can't remember what it was exactly."

"Then perhaps you can remember this. How long did you stay in the office with your wife?"

"Perhaps five, maybe ten minutes. I can't remember exactly."

"And when you left, was she still alive?"

There was a small silence.

The witness looked at me and seemed to catch his breath. Then he gave us the invariably charming smile.

"Of course she was."

"You spoke to Mr Luttrell at the reception area on your way out?"

"I did, yes."

"He says you asked him if Hussein Khan was in the building?"

"Yes, I did."

"Why did you do that?"

"I suppose I'd heard from someone that he might have been there."

"And what did Mr Luttrell tell you?"

"He said that Khan was in the building, yes."

"You knew that Hussein Khan's presence in that building was a potential danger to your wife."

"I suppose I knew. Yes."

"I suppose you did. And yet you left and drove off in your car without warning her?"

There was a longer silence then and Ricky's smile seemed to droop.

"I didn't go back to the office, no."

"Why not, Mr Glossop? Why not warn her? Why didn't you see that Khan left before you went off?"

And then Ricky Glossop said something which changed the atmosphere in court in a moment, even silencing the judge.

"I suppose I was in a hurry. I was on my way to a party."

After a suitable pause I asked, "There was no lock on your wife's office door, was there?"

"There might have been. But she never locked it."

"So you left her unprotected, with the man who had threatened her life still in the building, because you were on your way to a party?"

The smile came again, but it had no effect now on the jury.

"I think I heard he was with the senior tutor in the library. I suppose I thought that was safe."

"Mr Glossop, were you not worried by the possibility that the senior tutor might leave first, leaving the man who threatened your wife still in the building with her?"

"I suppose I didn't think of that," was all he could say.

I let the answer sink in and then turned to more dangerous and uncharted territory.

"I believe you're interested in various country sports."

"That's right, My Lord." The witness, seeming to feel the ground was now safer, smiled at the judge.

"You used to go shooting, I believe."

"Well, I go shooting, Mr Rumpole." A ghastly twitch of the lips was, from the bench, Graves's concession towards a smile. "And I hope you're not accusing me of complicity in any sort of a crime?"

I let the jury have their sycophantic laugh, then went on to ask, "Did you ever belong to a pistol shooting club, Mr Glossop?" Fig Newton, the private eye, had done his work well.

"When such clubs were legal, yes."

"And do you still own a handgun?"

"Certainly not." The witness seemed enraged. "I wouldn't do anything that broke the law."

I turned to look at the jury with my eyebrows raised, but for the moment the witness was saved by the bell as the judge announced that he could see by the clock that it was time we broke for lunch.

Before we parted, however, Soapy Sam got up to tell us that his next witness would be Mrs Glossop's secretary, Sue Blackmore, who would merely give evidence about the receipt of the letter and the deceased's reaction to it. Miss Blackmore was, apparently, likely to be a very nervous witness, and perhaps his learned friend Mr Rumpole would agree to her evidence being read.

Mr Rumpole did not agree. Mr Rumpole wanted Miss Sue Blackmore to be present in the flesh and he was ready to cross-examine her at length. And so we parted, expecting the trial of Hussein Khan for murder to start again at two o'clock.

But Khan's trial for murder didn't start again at two o'clock or at any other time. I was toying with a plate of steak and kidney pie and a pint of Guinness in the pub opposite the Old Bailey when I saw the furtive figure of Sam Ballard oozing through the crowd. He came to me obviously heavy with news.

"Rumpole! You don't drink at lunchtime, do you?"

"Yes. But not too much at lunchtime. Can I buy you a pint of stout?"

"Certainly not, Rumpole. Mineral water, if you have to. And could we move to that little table in the corner? This is news for your ears alone."

After I had transported my lunch to a more secluded spot and supplied our Head of Chambers with mineral water, he brought me up to date on that lunch hour's developments.

"It's Sue, the secretary, Rumpole. When we told her that

she'd have to go into the witness box, she panicked and asked to see Superintendent Gregory. By this time, she was in tears and, he told me, almost incomprehensible. However, Gregory managed to calm her down and she said she knew you'd get it out of her in the witness box, so she might as well confess that she was the one who had made the telephone call."

"Which telephone call was that?"

Soapy Sam was demonstrating his usual talent for making a simple statement of fact utterly confusing.

"The telephone call to your client. Telling him to go and meet the senior tutor."

"You mean . . . ?" The mists that had hung over the case of Khan the terrorist were beginning to clear. "She pretended to be . . ."

"The senior tutor's secretary. Yes. The idea was to get Khan into the building whilst Glossop . . ."

"Murdered his wife?" I spoke the words that Ballard seemed reluctant to use.

"I think she's prepared to give evidence against him," Soapy Sam said, looking thoughtfully towards future briefs. "Well, she'll have to, unless she wants to go to prison as an accessory."

"Has handsome Ricky heard the news yet?" I wondered.

"Mr Glossop has been detained. He's helping the police with their inquiries."

So many people I know, who help the police with their inquiries, are in dire need of help themselves. "So you'll agree to a verdict of not guilty of murder?" I asked Ballard, as though it was a request to pass the mustard.

"Perhaps. Eventually. And you'll agree to guilty of making death threats in a letter?"

"Oh, yes," I admitted. "We'll have to plead guilty to that."

But there was no hurry. I could finish my steak and kidney and order another Guinness in peace.

"It started off," I was telling Hilda over a glass of Château Thames Embankment that evening, "as an act of terrorism, of mad, religious fanaticism, of what has become the new terror of our times. And it ends up as an old-fashioned murder by a man who wanted to dispose of his rich wife for her money and be free to marry a pretty young woman. It was a case, you might say, of Dr Crippen meeting Osama Bin Laden."

"It's hard to say which is worse." She Who Must Be Obeyed was thoughtful.

"Both of them," I told her. "Both of them are worse. But I suppose we understand Dr Crippen better. Only one thing we can be grateful for."

"What's that, Rumpole?"

"The terrorist got a fair trial. And the whole truth came out in the end. The day when a suspected terrorist doesn't get a fair trial will be the day they've won the battle."

I refilled our glasses, having delivered my own particular verdict on the terrible events of that night at William Morris University.

"Mind you," I said, "it was your friend Gerald Graves who put me on to the truth of the matter."

"Oh, really." Hilda sounded unusually cool on the subject of the judge.

"It was when he was playing Father Christmas. He was standing in for someone else. And I thought, what if the real murderer thought he'd stand in for someone else. Hussein Khan had uttered the death threat and was there to take the blame. All Ricky had to do was go to work quickly. So that's what he did—he committed murder in Hussein Khan's name. That death threat was a gift from heaven for him."

One of our usual silences fell between us, and then Hilda said, "I don't know why you call Mr Justice Graves my friend."

"You got on so well at Christmas."

"Well, yes we did. And then he said we must keep in touch. So I telephoned his clerk and the message came back that the judge was busy for months ahead but he hoped we might meet again eventually. I have to tell you, Rumpole, that precious judge of yours does not treat women well."

I did my best. I tried to think of The Old Gravestone as a heartbreaker, a sort of Don Juan who picked women up and dropped them without mercy, but I failed miserably.

"I'm better off with you, Rumpole," Hilda told me. "I can always rely on you to be unreliable."